WAR WITHOUT FRIENDS

Evert Hartman

*Translated from the Dutch
by Patricia Crampton*

CROWN PUBLISHERS, INC.
New York

Copyright © 1979 by Lemniscaat b.v. Rotterdam
English translation copyright © 1982 by Patricia Crampton
All rights reserved. No part of this publication may be reproduced,
stored in a retrieval system, or transmitted, in any form or by any means,
electronic, mechanical, photocopying, recording, or otherwise, without
prior written permission of the publisher. Inquiries should be addressed
to Crown Publishers, Inc., One Park Avenue, New York, N.Y. 10016
First American edition 1982 by Crown Publishers, Inc.
Originally published in Dutch as Oorlog Zonder Vrienden
Manufactured in the United States of America
Published simultaneously in Canada by General Publishing Company Limited
10   9   8   7   6   5   4   3   2   1
The text of this book is set in 10 pt. Primer.

Library of Congress Cataloging in Publication Data
Hartman, Evert.
War without friends.
Translation of: Oorlog zonder vrienden.
Summary: In a small Dutch town during World War II,
fourteen-year-old Arnold, a member of the Hitler youth,
feels increasingly isolated and trapped between his
father's fervent support of the Nazi party and his
classmates' hostile opposition to all the Nazis stand for.
[1. World War, 1939–1945—Netherlands—Fiction.
2. Netherlands—History—German occupation, 1940–
1945—Fiction]   I. Title.
PZ7.H26732War   1982   [Fic]   82-10093
ISBN 0-517-54754-6

WAR WITHOUT FRIENDS

CHAPTER ONE ✄

Thursday, April 30, 1942

ARNOLD shouldn't have said it. His back to the school wall, he watched the three sturdily built boys close in on him, the look in their eyes anything but friendly.

"Say that again!" The middle boy's voice was hoarse with anger. Arnold was no coward, but there was not much point in starting a fight that was lost in advance. He edged his right foot up and back, so he could push off from the wall if necessary, but he said nothing.

The blond boy was almost within arm's reach when he repeated deliberately, "Say that again, you dirty Nazi!"

Arnold stiffened. He saw the menacing trio facing him, their eyes filled with the hatred that had led them in the last few months to insult and harass him and make his life a misery, all because his father was a member of the NSB, the Dutch National Socialist Movement. His parents had told him that if he ignored them they would stop, that a good National Socialist must be able to control himself. But there was a limit to self-control.

"You heard me." His voice was no more than a strangled whisper.

The boys crowded in on him. "We want to hear you again!"

Arnold pressed his lips together. He was looking at his classmates through a mist, but his foot was braced firmly against the wall. He said as calmly as possible: "If you think Queen Wilhelmina is going to do anything for you, you're a bunch of idiots."

The biggest boy shot out a fist, and even as he ducked, Arnold knew he was too late. The knuckles hit him close to the collarbone. A fierce pain shot through his shoulder, numbing his arm, but his anger was even greater than the pain. He kicked and lashed out until a vicious kick on the ankle made him stagger. He took a couple of desperate steps toward the gate, but a hard blow to the face made flight impossible. Someone tripped him and he fell.

It was an unequal struggle. They kicked his legs, punched his back and twisted his arms until he screamed with pain and fear. Then one of them grabbed him by the hair and pulled his head back, ready to smash it against the pavement.

"Boys!"

No one had noticed the tall, thin man in the doorway, but his voice struck them like a whip.

"Stop that at once!"

"The head," Arnold heard someone hiss. "Let's go!"

He felt them let go of him and get ready to run, but the headmaster had reached them in two long strides. "Martin, Johan and Hans—go to my room."

"He started it," Martin objected. "He insulted the queen."

The head did not raise his voice, but there was no friendliness in his eyes either. "Did you hear me, boys?"

As Arnold struggled to his feet he saw the three trudging toward the school door.

"And you"—the head's voice was expressionless—"go and wash and then wait for me in the corridor. Understand?"

Arnold did not answer. He rubbed his aching face, and a

broad streak of blood appeared on the back of his hand. He stared at it without interest and seemed scarcely to feel the pain in his arms and back. He felt only anger. He looked straight at the headmaster and said, "I'm going home."

The headmaster gripped him by the arm. "I told you to stay here. I want to know exactly what happened."

Arnold wrenched himself away at the cost of two more scratches, but the tears in his eyes were not tears of pain. "You wouldn't believe me anyway!" he shouted. "You can go to hell! I'm going home!" The next minute he was at the bicycle shed, had taken his bicycle and shot out of the school grounds.

He rode through the sunny streets like a madman, careless of the curious glances and pointed fingers. At last, panting, he flung his bicycle against the wall of his house, stumbled into the living room and burst into tears.

Mrs. Westervoort had the air of someone accustomed to the unexpected. She got up quickly, took his head in her hands and said simply, "My dear boy." Three seconds later she was in the kitchen, collecting a couple of wet cloths. She carefully wiped the dried blood off his upper lip, bathed his face and stroked back the wisps of hair from his sweaty forehead. Then she went back to the kitchen for a glass of water, which she set before him. She asked no questions, only repeating, "My dear boy."

It was some time before Arnold could say anything. "The bastards!" he said hoarsely.

"What happened, Arnold?" Mrs. Westervoort asked almost matter-of-factly, though her voice betrayed her anxiety.

"The bastards!" Arnold's sobs were not yet under control. "The dirty pigs! When I get my hands on them, I'll—I'll murder them!"

Her face was worried now. "If you could just try to tell me quietly what happened?"

[3]

"There were three of them. They beat me up. They—"

"Who?"

"Martin and Hans and Johan."

"Martin Jonkers?"

Arnold nodded. He held a cloth to his nose to stop another gush of blood.

"Why did they do that?" Mrs. Westervoort was annoyed as well as worried.

"We were talking about that woman in England and then—"

"Do you mean the queen?"

"The queen? You know as well as I do that she hasn't been queen for ages!"

"All right. So what did you say?"

"That they were stupid idiots if they thought that woman could still do anything for them."

She shook her head, looking grave. "You'd do much better to keep such things to yourself."

"Oh? Shouldn't I speak the truth, then?"

"It's sometimes very unwise to speak the truth. You should have held your tongue."

"I won't be bullied by a bunch of idiots!" He took the cloth from his nose and looked at the bloodstains. "I'm not going to school tomorrow."

She raised her eyebrows. "Why not?"

Arnold seemed not to have heard her. "I'll deal with them on Saturday . . . Saturday morning. . . ."

"I asked you why you don't want to go to school," said Mrs. Westervoort. "If the headmaster knew—"

"I told the head he could go to hell."

"*What* did you say?"

Arnold had stopped crying, but his voice was still shaking with anger. "The head wanted to see me, with those bastards. I refused. I said he could go to hell."

[4]

After a speechless moment, she whispered, "Did you really say that?"

He nodded.

Her voice was suddenly stern. "Then you'll go to school tomorrow, if only to apologize. You know how much trouble we had getting you into that school. And now you want to ruin everything? There'll be none of that. As for those boys, I shall . . ."

She stopped as Arnold got up. Although he was only just fourteen, he was almost as tall as she. He stood face to face with her, and she was alarmed at the look in his dark brown eyes. He said tightly, "I am not going to school tomorrow. Apologize? Never! They'd like that, the son of a Nazi apologizing, but I won't. I won't!" He struck the table with his fist and gasped at the pain that shot up his right side. He doubled up and collapsed into the chair.

"What is it, my boy?"

Arnold took a deep breath. "I think they kicked me in the ribs."

Mrs. Westervoort quickly unbuttoned his shirt and took it off; there were two deep, purplish welts, about eight inches below his armpit. "Perhaps we'd better put a bandage on that," she said, trying to speak calmly.

"Do you have to, Mom?" He put on his shirt. "You know I hate it. It'll pass anyway."

She hesitated. "What about your cheek?"

Arnold got up and went over to the mirror. The pain in his side was more bearable. "It's only a scratch," he said. "You always say things like that heal quicker without a dressing."

"Those boys, Martin and the others, did *they* go to the headmaster?" she asked.

"Yes." Arnold turned away from the mirror, walked to the window and stared out, his hands in his pockets.

"Then they will have had a good scolding."

"Then you don't know what goes on at school."

"What do you mean?"

"Oh, come on, Mom, you know! They've been baiting me for weeks and none of the teachers will lift a finger. That bunch will laugh themselves silly when they hear what's happened. As for the head, he's probably busy making a fuss of those pigs." He turned abruptly. "I can just hear him: 'Well, well, Martin . . . Hans . . . Johan . . . so you've been beating up Arnold? Well, you mustn't do it again, you know. That's not done at our school. We've got enough problems as it is. Now, you won't do it again, will you?' 'No, sir.' "

"Arnold!"

"Arnold what! It's the truth. The last time it happened was when that boy from Verdam—you know, that jerk in junior high—ran into me. He did it on purpose. I know he did. The headmaster was there watching. And do you know what he said? 'Gerard, be a bit careful with our ninth-grader.' I could have strangled him!"

"Don't be so quick-tempered, Arnold. How often have we told you you must control your temper? The angrier you get, the happier they are."

"*Let* them be. I just can't take it any longer!"

Mrs. Westervoort fiddled with the first-aid box, but said nothing. She looked up when she heard the sound of a bicycle being propped against the wall. "There's your dad."

A minute later, Mr. Westervoort came into the living room, a scrawny man with a pointed face, his dark blond hair combed straight back, gray patches at the temples. Despite the sunny spring weather, he was wearing a raincoat. He looked tired.

"You're early this afternoon." Mrs. Westervoort looked inquiringly at her husband. "Is something the matter?"

[6]

"A headache. I only left an hour earlier than usual. I'll make up for it another time."

"Was that all right with the others at the town hall?"

"It had to be." He started taking off his coat. "You don't think I still have to ask their permission, do you?"

She didn't answer.

"*I* decide when I come and go. It's not up to anyone else!" He threw his coat over the back of the chair and rubbed his eyes. "Just give me a cup of tea." He was about to sit down when he saw Arnold's face with the bloody scratch on his right cheek. "What happened to you?"

Arnold shrugged. "Oh, nothing. Ask Mom. Then I won't have to tell it all twice." He started to walk out of the room, but his father caught his arm.

"Just a minute, you. You know I won't stand for that kind of talk. What's the matter with you?" His voice was shaking.

Mrs. Westervoort stood up quickly. "Koos, please! The boy's gone through enough already."

"That's just what I want to know. So could I possibly have a proper answer?"

At first the words would not come. Then: "They had a fight," she said.

"Who had a fight?"

"Arnold and a couple of the other boys."

"Who were they?"

"Oh, that's not important."

"I asked who they were!"

"Well, Martin Jonkers and, er . . ."

"Johan Laning and Hans van Beek," finished Arnold. He looked as if he were thinking of something else.

"All three of them?" Mr. Westervoort's voice had roughened, but he was no longer grasping his son. "What was the fight about?"

"Same as usual." For a moment, Arnold looked his father in the eye. "They beat me up."

Mr. Westervoort seemed not to take the words in at first, then he grabbed his coat and stormed out of the room. Or was about to, but his wife barred the way.

"Koos, please, don't do anything foolish! The headmaster—"

"Do anything foolish! Who's the one who's being foolish around here?"

"For heaven's sake, don't get so excited!"

"I'm not getting excited," Mr. Westervoort hissed. "I've just about had enough of that boy being bullied day after day! I've had enough of being cold-shouldered. And I'm fed up with listening to the stupid sniggers of a pack of good-for-nothings at work. I'm fed up!" His voice was trembling with anger. "And I'm finally going to do something about it!" He pushed his wife aside and rushed down the hall and through the kitchen.

She caught up with him at the back door and tried frantically to hold him back. "Koos, just think for a minute. You're making life impossible for us. And we've so few friends left as it is!"

There was a strange gleam in Mr. Westervoort's eye. "We've got more friends than you think," he retorted. He opened the door, got on his bicycle and rode quickly away.

CHAPTER TWO ✐

DO hurry up, Arnold. If you're late you may get into more trouble." Mrs. Westervoort was standing at the kitchen table, cutting brown sticky slices of something that looked like bread. She looked pale and tired; her worried eyes revealed that she had slept badly. "Do you want your milk hot or cold?"

"Cold." Arnold tied his shoelaces and ran down the stairs. His face was gloomy, and he had the look of someone afraid of being caught doing something wrong. "Has Dad gone yet?"

"Yes."

"He's not usually that early."

She said hastily, "I think he wants to catch up on things today . . . you know he lost time yesterday."

"I was crazy to make such a fuss."

"Don't say that. You know what your father's like."

Arnold nodded and tried to get down a mouthful of bread.

"Do you want a sandwich to take with you?"

"As long as it doesn't have this disgusting syrup on it."

"I'll put some brown sugar on it."

"All right." He took a gulp or two of milk. "Is Rita awake yet?"

"No." Mrs. Westervoort went on making the sandwiches.

"Late home last night, wasn't she?"

"Did you hear her come home?"

"Did I?" he scoffed. "The whole street must have heard her! *I* would have caught hell had I come home that late!"

"You're not seventeen!" There was a moment's silence before she went on, "They brought her home."

"Who? Jürgen and Manfred? Those German soldiers?"

"Yes."

He grinned. "Oh, actually the same ones as last week!"

"Arnold!" She fiddled with the butter knife and smiled suddenly. "Well, your cheek's looking better already. Are your ribs bothering you?"

"Hardly at all. I didn't need that bandage, did I?"

She stroked his hair on her way to the cupboard. But as soon as she opened the cupboard door to get out the sugar, she knew she had made a mistake and shut it again, quickly.

But Arnold had seen. He stopped chewing. "Where did you get hold of those sausages?"

"Sausages?" Mrs. Westervoort started nervously spreading butter again. "Oh, I got those from . . ."

"They weren't there yesterday. Actually, since you're making me a sandwich anyway, I'd rather have a bit of sausage on it than that sweet stuff."

"The sausages are for tonight." She took a deep breath. "And for Sunday."

"I could do with a couple of slices," Arnold grumbled.

She looked at him uncertainly. "All right," she said at last. "I'll give you a bit. But you mustn't say—" She broke off in mid-sentence.

"Mustn't say what?"

[10]

"Oh, nothing—drop it. Anyway, we're wasting time. It's a quarter past eight and you're walking, aren't you?"

"Yes." Arnold washed down the last sticky bite of bread while he greedily watched his mother cut off half an inch of sausage and put it in his sandwich.

She held his shoulders. "I'm glad you're going to school after all."

He shrugged.

"You mustn't have anything to do with those boys," she said earnestly. "Will you promise, Arnold?"

"I'll do my best." He put on his jacket.

"Have you got your bag?"

"It's still at school. At least—if they haven't pinched it. Well, I'm off. See you this afternoon." Then he was in the street, walking in the direction of the school. At the point where he knew his mother could no longer see him, he ducked down a side street, toward the river, and slowed his pace to a casual saunter.

His father had come home at about six the evening before, saying nothing, even when his wife asked him where he had been. And until nine o'clock, when Arnold went to bed, he had sat reading the paper in silence. But Arnold had overheard a conversation when he had gone to the bathroom an hour or two later. He had sat on the stairs, holding his breath, listening.

"He shouldn't have anything to do with those boys." That was his mother.

He was surprised how calmly his father answered: "I would have started a fight, too, in his place."

"He didn't start it."

"Well, all right. I wouldn't have avoided a fight, either."

"They may treat him even worse next time."

"I don't think they'll dare."

"Then you don't know Martin Jonkers. Arnold's had trouble with him more than once before."

"Martin Jonkers?" Arnold heard the contempt in his father's voice. "After tomorrow, Martin Jonkers won't be making any trouble at all."

"How do you know? Did you go to Jonkers's bookshop this afternoon?"

"You surely don't think I'd set foot in there, do you? No, you just leave this kind of thing to me."

"I really worry about you sometimes."

"You don't have to worry about me." His father's voice sounded grumpy. "I'm just sick of being pushed around. We should all follow our Leader's example. He doesn't take things lying down! And that Jonkers scum has needed a lesson for some time. I sometimes wonder if the man's got Jewish blood. How else can you earn so much money from a miserable bookshop like that?"

"You don't know if he earns a lot."

"You're not going to stand up for him, are you?"

His mother had spoken so quietly then that Arnold could barely hear her. "No, of course not, but . . ."

"But what?"

"As long as nothing happens to you."

"It won't, don't you worry. That mob's in too much of a funk. And it's high time we showed them."

"What do you mean?"

"You'll see!"

The chairs scraped: They were getting up.

Seconds later, Arnold was in bed again, but he still couldn't sleep. At about half past twelve, his sister Rita's German friends had brought her home. They had stood outside talking loudly before saying good night. Then he had heard some more sounds from the kitchen, but was too tired to pay much attention.

[12]

Arnold walked on, wondering what his father had meant about Jonkers's bookshop. He passed the local commandant's headquarters with its swastika flag. Another hundred yards and he was in the side street where Jonkers's bookshop stood. Arnold walked past, pretending indifference, but squinting sidelong at it. He couldn't see anything unusual.

In five minutes he was at the river. A fresh northeasterly wind was blowing across the current, making the water choppy. Screaming sea gulls skimmed the water. Lounging along the quayside, he tried to think of some way of getting at Martin Jonkers and his friends. It wouldn't be easy. Martin Jonkers was the kind who was afraid of very little. And ever since the war began, his father had strictly forbidden him to do the easiest thing: tell the Gestapo. More than once he had heard him say: If it comes to that, I'll do it myself! Arnold didn't dare disobey his father.

About twenty minutes later he reached the edge of town, where the quay turned into a wide dike running beside the river with the railroad track more or less parallel to it, fifty yards away.

A milkman's horse and cart drew up level with him, the big empty cans rattling. Arnold walked faster to keep up. "Can you give me a ride?"

The man frowned at him before jerking his thumb over his shoulder in reply.

Arnold scrambled into the back of the cart and dangled his legs over the iron railing.

After jolting along for five minutes they reached the point where the road left the dike and the railroad track curved off to the south. Arnold jumped down. "Thanks!" he shouted, but there was no way of knowing whether the driver had heard or not.

Arnold watched the milkman disappear around a corner into the woods bordering the dike.

Then he took the narrower road along the dike, aimlessly kicking pebbles as he went. A hundred yards farther on, the road divided again: A recently tarred road led across the water meadow to a landing stage attached to the nearby quarry. Two ships were moored there. Men in gray-green uniforms were busily unloading crates; two German Wehrmacht motorbikes with sidecars were parked on the road by the jetty. Fifty yards inland from it stood a notice board: STRICTLY FORBIDDEN TO UN-AUTHORIZED PERSONS.

Arnold stopped.

The landscape was rather like a painting: the lazily flowing river, the grazing cows, a windmill on the outskirts of the town, and a clear blue sky arching over all. To the east, at any rate. The sky to the south and west was streaked with mare's tails. He was looking at these without interest when he suddenly spotted three arrow-shaped white streaks among the clouds— the unmistakable trail of three fighter planes. They were too high for the sound of their engines to be heard, however, and Arnold lost interest in them when the streaks vanished into nothingness. He was about to turn back to the public road when he heard someone call from the jetty. One of the German soldiers was beckoning him. "You, come here!"

For a minute, Arnold stayed where he was, undecided and a little wary.

"Don't be frightened!" shouted the soldier. "We won't eat you!"

Arnold walked slowly over to the group of soldiers. There were six of them he saw now, two in the hold passing crates up, two carrying them across the jetty and the other two stacking them five deep in rows. The last job was obviously the slowest; dozens of crates were still unstacked.

"Are you strong?" The soldier who had called spoke to him in German, grinning broadly. "Can you understand me?"

Arnold nodded.

"Can you help?" The soldier spoke with deliberate slowness.

Arnold pointed to his ribs. "Don't know. I'm hurt." He was not at all bad at German.

The German laughed jeeringly. He turned to another soldier who was just hoisting a crate onto the top layer. "Listen to this, Werner, there's a Hollander here who's already learned a few tricks!"

"What?"

Arnold started to lose his temper. "It's not a trick," he growled. "It's true!"

Amused, the first soldier pushed back his cap. "Let's see where it hurts," he said, laughing.

Arnold gritted his teeth. "No," he said. Going over to the crates, he lifted one. He neither knew nor cared what was in it. He noticed only that it had to weigh at least a hundred pounds. With muscles straining and a stabbing pain in his ribs, he walked with it to the pile and set it down with a bang on the third-highest row.

Both soldiers applauded. "Bravo, bravo! Well done." They pointed to the ship. "Only a hundred to go!"

Arnold did not answer. His right hand pressed to the sore place in his side, he returned to the crates on the ground. He would not give in. And he would show them that there were some Dutchmen who were not too poor-spirited to give German soldiers a hand.

For the first few minutes he tried to keep pace with the two soldiers, but when the sweat began pouring down his face he stopped. Panting, he fished a handkerchief out of his pocket and wiped his forehead.

That was when he saw the planes. There were three, coming

from the southwest. Normally they would have heard the engines, but the stiff northeaster blew the sound away. He pointed, almost hesitantly, at the fighters rushing toward them.

"Planes," he said.

The soldier called Werner looked up from his work.

"What!" The next second he had flung down the crate he was carrying. "Damnation!" he shouted. *"Planes!* Take cover!"

CHAPTER THREE ⚑

IF he had reacted immediately, Arnold might have been able to get away. As it was, he stood rooted to the spot, watching the oncoming British fighters, until one of the German soldiers pushed him roughly to the ground. The next moment five of them were lying flat behind the pile of crates.

The first thing he heard was a high whine that quickly swelled to an ear-splitting scream. Then all hell broke loose. Rattling machine guns sent down a stream of bullets that spattered on the quayside like hailstones, piercing the ships and sending up fountains of water. As the shadow of the machine passed over them, the noise changed from a scream to a deafening roar. The lead plane skimmed the river, climbed fast and began to make a wide turn.

His face rigid against the concrete, Arnold heard the next fighter coming, followed almost immediately by the third. He smelled the penetrating stink of exhaust fumes. The fear rose in his throat.

Two new showers of bullets drowned all thought. He knew it

was over only when he heard the soldiers beside him shouting above the booming of the engines.

One of the soldiers who had been working on the ship climbed out of the hold and ran to the fo'c'sle. He snatched away a tarpaulin, and a moment later he was kneeling behind a machine gun, which he swung to the southwest. He was just in time: The first fighter was beginning its second dive. Arnold went on watching the soldier taking aim until he was forced down again. "Take cover, you fool!"

The machine gun on the ship rattled before the British pilot had his plane on course, which was probably why the next stream of bullets struck a little to one side of them. But the second and third were much closer. Bullets ricocheted off the stones; wood splinters flew up. Two of the topmost crates wobbled, spun around and crashed to the ground next to Arnold.

It was only when he looked up for the second time that he could clearly see the damage the British had done. The ship carrying the crates had been riddled through and through and was tilting slowly. The bridge was in ruins. Half the rudder had disappeared. Arnold stared after the planes, despite his fear that they might come back a third time. But the fighters were tearing upward at high speed, except for the last one. He watched a fast-growing plume of smoke trailing behind it. The machine made an uncertain turn, as if the pilot were no longer in control, and suddenly burst into orange flames. It began to lose height. Arnold watched breathlessly as a tiny figure detached itself from the burning fighter. A white parachute unfolded and sailed with the wind in the direction of the wood. The fighter was falling fast, a ball of fire and smoke. Three seconds later, it crashed into the river five hundred yards away. The flames were quenched. Oily smoke drifted across the water.

The Germans showed hardly any interest. While Arnold stood watching the spectacle, they were running wildly to the sinking ship. "Hurry! Klaus, he's been hurt!" They struggled over the broken crates in the gangway to the fo'c'sle, where the limp body of a German soldier hung from his machine gun. Two of them quickly dragged him off the deck and onto the landing stage. They were just in time. The ship heeled over steeply, until it was hanging on mooring ropes stretched taut as violin strings. Half the deck was underwater.

As Arnold scrambled to his feet, he heard the air-raid sirens wailing from the town. The British pilot drifted away with his parachute and finally disappeared behind the top of the dike, somewhere in the woods.

When Arnold turned around, he saw the soldiers bending over the still body of their friend. He heard Werner say in a faint voice, "He's dead." And then, a moment later, yelling, "My God, he's dead!" He shook his fists at the sky in impotent fury. "Damned dirty pig, you'll regret this!" Raging, he returned to the others. Arnold saw the tears in his eyes. "Let's go and look for the pilot," he said hoarsely.

The soldiers wasted no time. They ran to the motorbikes that were standing ready, seized their guns from the sidecars and kicked the starters. One engine obeyed at once but the other stayed silent; a bullet had pierced the cylinder. A truck came roaring toward them from the direction of the town, took the bend dangerously and braked a few yards from the group. In the back, Arnold saw at least ten helmeted soldiers, rifles between their knees. The man next to the driver climbed down from the cab, taking in the chaos at a glance. After exchanging a few quick words, he got in again. Then he saw Arnold.

"Who's the boy?"

"He's been helping us."

The soldier turned piercing gray eyes on him. "Did you see the pilot?"

Arnold nodded. His heart was beating fast.

"I mean—where did he land?"

Arnold felt his legs trembling. He pointed a bit uncertainly into the distance. "In the wood," he said.

"Will you show us the way?"

"Yes."

The German jerked his head. "Come with us!"

They pushed him onto the motorbike behind Werner's broad back. Another soldier got into the sidecar. Arnold had to hold on tightly as the machine snorted up the dike.

They reached the junction. "Left!" he shouted in Werner's ear, and then, after two hundred yards, "Right here!"

The motorbike shot up the woodland track, followed by the army truck. Arnold stayed on with great difficulty as Werner raced through the wood as if there were no bumps or hollows. The drive lasted only a few minutes, but Arnold felt shaken to pieces by the time they reached a clearing. "Stop!" he shouted. Werner turned the motorbike onto the grass. The army truck arrived a moment later.

"I saw him come down here somewhere," Arnold said.

"What?"

"He must be here."

"Good."

Brief orders were shouted, and the Germans began grimly to search the woods. One soldier stayed behind to guard the vehicles.

Arnold stayed there too, his mind in a whirl. How long ago had he left home? One hour? Two? He didn't know. Too much had happened. He was only just beginning to realize how lucky he'd been. So it was true what they said—what his father had said too: The British shot everything in sight, without considering whether innocent people were the victims. He had heard of large cities being bombed, killing hundreds of people.

They were right: The attacks were cowardly. He could still visualize the motionless body of the soldier they'd called Klaus. How old had he been—twenty or so, maybe? He hadn't stood a chance. It was amazing that he'd managed to hit one of the British planes. Arnold hoped the man who had jumped out would be found quickly and get what was coming to him. Down the path came a cyclist with some milk cans in a small wagon. When he saw the truck and motorbike he tried to pedal quickly past, but the soldier had seen him.

"*Halt!*" He raised his rifle.

The farmer stopped, his eyes fearful.

"Who are you?"

The cyclist shook his head, bewildered. "I haven't done anything."

The German hesitated, then beckoned Arnold. "You—come here. Who is this man?"

Arnold felt uneasy. He'd seen the man before. He probably lived in one of the farms behind the wood and had been collecting the cans left at the roadside by the milkman. "He lives around here," he said. "A farmer."

The soldier waved his gun. "All right. Move along."

The farmer didn't hesitate. He threw a frightened glance at Arnold and hurried away.

It was another five minutes before they found the pilot. There were excited shouts in the distance; shortly afterward six men came out of the woods.

The British pilot looked bad. His face was covered with scratches, his torn uniform sticky with blood and he was limping slightly. But his young face was proud. By the truck he dropped his raised hands.

"Hands up!" snarled one of the Germans.

But the Englishman pretended not to hear and climbed into the back of the truck, where he started to loosen his shoelaces.

In a few minutes the other soldiers returned, and Werner saw the pilot. At once he was in the truck and had him by the throat.

"You did it," he hissed. "You English pig!" He had balled his fist for a punch when the commandant's voice barked, "Stop that!"

Werner took a deep breath and dropped his hand.

"The Englishman is a prisoner of war," the other snapped. "Get down!"

The soldier slowly climbed down from the truck, walked over to his motorbike and kicked down furiously on the starter. Two others got on with him and the motorbike shot away.

The remaining soldiers clambered into the army truck. The commandant stuck his head out of the cab. "Want a lift?" he called.

Arnold shook his head. He watched the truck turn. Grass and earth flew out from under the rear wheels as the driver accelerated. The soldiers and their prisoner lurched to and fro. Suddenly they were around a bend and out of sight. There was nothing left but the fading growl of engines.

Arnold suddenly felt tired. His legs were still trembling and there was a constriction in his throat that he could not swallow down. He walked over to a fallen tree and sat on it, his head in his hands.

He had done well to show the soldiers the way. He was sure of that. After all, the British were the Netherlands' greatest enemies, weren't they? Mussert, their Leader, had said so: enemies of the Fatherland. And Arnold had sworn faith to his Fatherland in the Jeugdstorm, the Nazi youth movement, not long ago. He and his comrades had pledged themselves to defend their Fatherland, to the death if necessary. Wasn't that what had just happened? He had been under a hail of bullets but he hadn't been hit. Was it a miracle? Or the guidance of a higher power?

He looked up at the peacefully rustling treetops. They suddenly reminded him of the most important Jeugdstorm motto: "In God we trust; all for the Fatherland." Now he knew what that "all" meant: He had to do his utmost for the Fatherland, however difficult it was. Even if bullying and suspicion were hell for him.

He had actually heard someone from the movement say over the radio: "Your family will curse you, your friends will avoid you, colleagues will pretend you don't exist. You will be alone, at home, at work and in church."

His father had often quoted those words, adding that that was why they would find true, loyal friends only within their National Socialist Party. Besides, they were lucky to have such powerful friends and protectors. He had discovered that for himself. If Werner hadn't pulled him down . . .

He got up and walked toward the road. He still had no idea of the time, but he could safely go home during school hours. There was no longer any need to fear a scolding. In fact, it was a good thing he hadn't gone to school.

He left the woods behind. A group of people was standing on the dike opposite the landing stage, holding bicycles. The milkman was there, too, his cart now empty. "Poor devil," he heard him say, "did you see him sitting there with the Nazis? If you ask me, they'd beaten him up, all ten of them. And yet they call themselves the Master Race. They're not masters, they're bastards!" But his voice was gleeful as he went on, "Look what they got for it, though!" He pointed to the wrecked ship. "That's not much good to anyone now." He got back into the cart and urged his horse on. "A few more jobs like that," he said over his shoulder, "and they'll have cracked the Nazis!" He caught sight of Arnold. "Hey," he called, almost cheerfully, "want another ride?"

Arnold did not even try to control himself. "No!" he snarled. "I'll find some other company!"

He knew at once that he shouldn't have said it. They stared at him, first in amazement, then with fear and suspicion. Without another word the group broke up and they all cycled away.

The milkman drove off toward the town, urging his horse on with a whip that Arnold had not seen him use earlier that day.

It was nearly eleven when Arnold walked into the kitchen. His sister Rita was at the table, a half-empty breakfast plate in front of her.

"My, you're early," she greeted him, her mouth full.

"Can't say the same for you!" he snapped back.

"Don't flare up! Or have you been beaten up again? Couldn't keep that big mouth of yours shut, I suppose?"

"*You* can't talk about big mouths—"

He heard his mother's voice from upstairs. "Who's that, Rita?"

"Me!" he called before his sister could answer.

"You, Arnold? Already?" Mrs. Westervoort hurried downstairs, her face still anxious. "What's happened? Have you been sent home?"

Arnold came out of the kitchen. "I haven't been to school."

"What? Where have you been all this time, then?"

He did not answer at once.

"Arnold, speak up! You haven't done anything foolish, have you?"

He shook his head again. "No, I don't think so." He smiled vaguely at his mother. "I went for a walk, outside town."

Rita came out of the kitchen to listen.

"Outside town? What on earth were you doing there? There was an air-raid warning. Why didn't you come home at once? Didn't you hear the shooting?"

Arnold looked at his mother and then at his sister. "They were shooting at me, too," he said.

If he had meant to frighten his mother, he had gone about it the right way. Mrs. Westervoort turned pale and clutched the back of a chair. Almost inaudibly, she whispered, *"What* did you say?"

Arnold tried to sound nonchalant. "There were some soldiers working at the jetty," he explained, "down by the quarry, you know. They were unloading a ship. I helped them. Then these planes suddenly appeared." He saw the deathly fear in his mother's eyes and added, rather unnecessarily, "I wasn't hit." After a moment's silence he went on, "But they shot down one plane, and we went to look for the pilot."

"We? You mean you went, too?"

"Well, they asked me to help."

"Could you understand them?" Rita teased.

"Oh, get lost! I'm not as dense as you are!"

She gave a peal of laughter. "He's off again!"

Mrs. Westervoort shook her head slowly, turned and left the room.

Mr. Westervoort came home at a quarter past twelve. He was in an excellent mood, but there was a tension about him, as if something awful might happen at any moment.

Five minutes later he had heard Arnold's story. He was quiet for some time. Then he spoke very seriously: "It was wrong of you, Arnold, not to go to school. But you did the right thing. You showed the Germans that they do have real allies in the Netherlands. And above all you helped to defend our Fatherland against a cowardly attack. What you did was dangerous, but I'm proud of you. If everyone in our movement was like that, we'd be able to defeat the most powerful enemy together."

Arnold felt his color rising as his father laid a hand on his shoulder. "What about school?" he asked, stammering slightly. "Do I have to go this afternoon?"

Mr. Westervoort smiled. "I dare say a couple of hours won't make much difference. Read a good book or something. You'll go tomorrow, though. Agreed—comrade?"

Arnold nodded. His voice sounded strange as he repeated, "Agreed."

CHAPTER FOUR 🐦

ARNOLD felt gloomy and a little frightened on the way to school next morning. What was the headmaster going to say? After all, he had been absent. And he'd been rude, too. He might be able to excuse his absence by saying he hadn't felt well, but what about his rudeness to the head?

At twenty-five past eight, nervous and reluctant, he walked into the school grounds. The boys in his class were in the bicycle shed, apparently deep in conversation. Martin Jonkers wasn't there, but he spotted Johan Laning and Hans van Beek at once. He headed quickly for the school entrance, but the group seemed to sense his presence, because they all suddenly turned toward him. The conversation stopped. Johan Laning stuck his hands in his trouser pockets, grinning.

"Hello, Arnold!" he said. The words rang out over the school grounds. Grins appeared on other faces.

Arnold felt still more uncertain. Were they up to something? If so, what? Maybe they'd found his bag and had taken something from it, or maybe they were going to accept him after all. Had the head or one of the teachers intervened? If so, it could only have been Mr. Dijkman, the history teacher. He was one of the few who had never been mean to him.

"Hello, Arnold." This time it was Hans van Beek.

Arnold did not know what to do. This cheery greeting from a boy with whom he'd just been in a fight was the last thing he would have expected. Maybe they were a bit frightened? Only—there was no trace of fear on Hans's cheerful face.

Arnold stopped and smiled awkwardly at him.

"Hello, Arnold." Someone else now.

Perhaps they had decided not to play any more games. He answered weakly, "Hello."

They had been waiting for that. The group exploded with merriment. Roaring with laughter, they staggered among the bicycle racks, clutching one another for support and slapping one another on the back.

Arnold stiffened, a feeling of icy cold creeping upward from the pit of his stomach, his hands clammy. He turned abruptly and walked over to the school. More shouts followed him, but he did not hear them.

He was taking off his coat and hanging it angrily on the hook when the headmaster suddenly appeared beside him.

"Good morning, Arnold."

Startled, he blinked at the headmaster without answering.

The headmaster looked sharply at him. "Why weren't you at school yesterday?" he asked quietly.

Arnold took a deep breath. From the corridors came the noise of boys and girls going to their classrooms. He said, "I, er, I didn't feel too good."

"Because of the fight, do you think?"

He shrugged. "Maybe."

"So you stayed home all day yesterday?"

Arnold was on his guard at once. Why had the headmaster asked that? Could he have seen him yesterday morning? Or had he heard something? He answered cautiously, "No, sir, I—er—I went for a short walk. My mother thought it would do me good."

The headmaster continued to watch him with cool gray eyes. "Have you brought a note from your parents?"

"No, sir."

"Why not?"

"I forgot, sir." He stole a glance down the corridor where his classmates were jostling up the stairs.

"Is that all you have to say to me, Arnold?"

"Yes, sir."

"Are you sure?"

Arnold's lips tightened. He nodded.

"All right then, Arnold, go to your class. Your bag is with the porter."

"Yes, sir." Arnold felt the sweat prickle on his neck. He hurried to the porter's office, and the man sourly passed him his book bag. In two minutes he was at his place, on the left by the window.

The class was still laughing, but they all stopped when Mr. Dijkman came in.

"Good morning, everyone."

"Good morning, sir."

Mr. Dijkman walked to the teacher's desk, put down his bag and took out the Bible. "We shall begin at once," he said, "because we have a lot to get through this morning. I am going to read you Psalm Eighty-three."

He waited until everyone was quiet, and then his low but carrying voice filled the room:

"A song or Psalm of Asaph.
Keep not thou silence, O God: hold not thy peace, and be not still, O God.

For, lo, thine enemies make a tumult: and they that hate thee have lifted up the head.

They have taken crafty counsel against thy people, and consulted against thy hidden ones.

They have said, Come, and let us cut them off from being a nation; that the name of Israel may be no more in remembrance."

Arnold only half listened to the catalog of the people intent on destroying Israel. He stared out the window at the bushes outside. A woman was walking her dog. On the road behind, a bus rattled by.

"So persecute them with thy tempest," he heard Mr. Dijkman read out. "Let them be confounded and troubled for ever."

Arnold's senses were suddenly alerted. Peering cautiously over his shoulder, he found a number of boys and girls looking mockingly in his direction. He turned back to the teacher as he closed his Bible, but he could see nothing unusual in Mr. Dijkman's manner as he folded his hands and said a simple prayer.

The "Amen" was swiftly followed by the noise of bags and books being put out on desks.

Mr. Dijkman looked around the class. "Does anyone happen to know where Martin Jonkers is?"

Hans van Beek lifted his head. "Don't you know, then?"

"What should I know?"

"They ransacked Jonkers's shop, last night. I think Martin's helping clear up the mess."

Arnold did not move, but his head was suddenly whirling. Jonkers's bookshop ransacked? Who could have done it? He had heard nothing. Could his father have meant something like that when he stormed out of the house on Thursday afternoon? Or were there other reasons?

[30]

"Do you also know who did it?" asked Mr. Dijkman.

Hans hesitated. "My father says they were—er—NSBers, Nazis. At least, they were wearing black uniforms."

"WA men," said Mr. Dijkman. With a set face he added, "These things happen nowadays. I just hope none of you get mixed up in it."

In the silence that followed, one or two people tittered.

"Who thinks this is something to laugh about?"

Nobody moved.

"Was it you, Johan?"

"No, sir."

Mr. Dijkman said sharply, "Never laugh at things like this. Right?"

"We weren't laughing because of what happened in the shop," said a girl in the back row; "it was something else."

"Could you tell me what, Marloes?"

"I'd rather not, sir."

Arnold looked out of the window again, seeing nothing, no bushes, no street, his heart beating wildly. He knew only too well why they had been tittering, but did Mr. Dijkman? Was he playing games? He heard the teacher say, "All right, Marloes, we'll say no more about it. Open your books at paragraph 1 5," he went on immediately, "then we'll see whether the Hapsburgs succeeded in seizing power in Europe."

The lesson continued without further incident, but Arnold was unable to concentrate. So Martin Jonkers had got his just deserts; his father, too. He ought to be happy but he wasn't.

After the bell for the second period he shuffled silently behind the others to the math class. It was more boisterous than the history lesson, and after only five minutes a paper dart landed on Arnold's desk. He looked round quickly to see who had thrown it, but his classmates were staring innocently at the blackboard.

Arnold unfolded the paper and read:

A stinker in the NSB
Sees only what the Nazis see,
And leads his "comrades" by the hand,
Off to betray the Fatherland.
"Look, there's a pilot in the wood!
Come on, you fellows, shoot him good!
If someone gives me any trouble,
I'll get his shop reduced to rubble!"
An NSBer, Nazi dog,
Stinks worse than any open bog!

The math teacher seemed suddenly aware that it was quieter than usual. He looked around the class until he saw Arnold. "Is there anything wrong, Arnold?" he asked.

"I don't feel very well, sir. Please may I go to the bathroom?"

"Go ahead."

He left his desk and went to the door. The eyes of twenty-five students bored into his back like red-hot needles. Then he shut the door. Behind him the clamor started up again.

There was no one in the corridor, and his rapid footsteps sounded loud and hollow. He locked himself in the bathroom, fished the paper out of his pocket, tore it up, dropped the pieces in the bowl and flushed them away.

He did it all automatically, blazing with incredible rage. The dirty pigs! The bastards! He could murder them. They had been at it all morning.

Hot tears burned behind his eyelids as he turned around. Then he saw what had been scrawled on the lavatory door: "H A L T. Hang All Lousy Traitors." Again he felt that suffocating spasm which made it almost impossible to breathe. The swine! No one did anything about it, not even the teachers. All they did was read pious extracts while the class listened with hypocritical expressions. Just like church. They preached about love there, but on the way out they spat at your feet.

Arnold waited a minute before returning to the classroom.

The class went quiet at once. The teacher looked questioningly at him. "Do you feel a bit better now?"

He answered loudly, "Much better, sir. I've just flushed away some filth."

The master looked strangely at him and turned back to the equations on the board.

The class was more subdued than usual.

They must have been taken aback by Arnold's venomous answer because nothing else happened until the Dutch lesson, the last that morning. Fifteen minutes before the bell, the teacher unsuspectingly turned the blackboard over. Even someone with bad eyesight could read it: "NSB—NSBer—NSBeast."

The class howled with laughter.

The teacher glanced uncertainly at Arnold, grabbed the eraser and rubbed the words out.

Then he said sternly, "Whoever wrote this nonsense will report to me at the end of the class!"

Silence fell again at once, but the teacher felt there was little point in continuing the lesson.

Barely ten minutes later they swarmed out, leaving Arnold in peace.

The teacher was left alone.

CHAPTER FIVE ◢

"AVEN'T you got any homework for Monday?" Mrs. Westervoort asked Arnold.

His hand was on the doorknob. "Oh, I'll do it tomorrow."

"On Sunday?"

"What do I care! Anyway, I can spend the time we used to spend sitting in church on my homework now."

She did not answer.

Arnold felt he had won a small victory. "Well," he said, "I'm off, then."

He opened the door.

"Where are you going?"

"Oh—around."

"Not back to the landing stage?"

"No."

"Will you be careful?"

He sighed. "I can just about manage to look after myself! You see danger everywhere." He saw the worry in her dark eyes. "I might even go to the Jeugdstorm for a while," he added.

"Shouldn't you put your uniform on, then?"

[34]

"No. If I need it, I'll come back for it."

"Well, all right. What time will you be home?"

"Around five, I expect."

She nodded. "Take care."

He stepped into the street and closed the door behind him. The clock on the Westerkerk tower showed a quarter past two.

It was rather cold, with a fine drizzle falling from gray clouds. Arnold turned up his collar and walked into town. Toward the center it grew busier—luckily for him, because he didn't want to be noticed. He passed a draper's shop where customers were crowding around the counter with coupons in their hands. A little farther on, a group of German soldiers stood talking. Most people were giving them a wide berth.

Ten minutes later, he came to the street where Jonkers's bookshop stood. He walked on until he was within thirty yards of the shop. Then he stopped, apparently interested in a window display on the other side. But the reflection in the windowpane gave him an excellent view; that is, he saw a shop with boarded-up windows. The shop door was out of sight, but he had no doubt that it would look much the same. The WA men had done a good job!

Arnold felt no sympathy. They had asked for it, the bullies. And if Johan Laning didn't watch out, he'd get what was coming to him, too. He was sorry now that he had thrown that paper away. He might have been able to use it as proof.

Warily, he moved ten yards on, to the next shop. It sold fishing tackle, so he could stay there quietly for a time without arousing suspicion. Now and again he glanced quickly over his shoulder, but could only see that the paving stones in front of the bookshop were blackened. They had probably burned a pile of books in the street. The WA men must have found some forbidden reading matter. Hadn't he heard his father say that

Jonkers probably had Jewish blood? If so, it was a good thing they had taken the bastards in hand. After all, you couldn't be hard enough on that kind of scum. And it was a sensible rule that Jews could no longer go everywhere. There had recently been an article in the *Nationaal Dagblad* about the beach, one of the places now forbidden to Jews. "The North Sea will no longer have to wash greasy Jewish flesh," he'd read, "and the glories of Germanic Nature will be protected from the immorality and vandalism of people who belong in the desert. . . ."

They wouldn't like it, of course, but it was their own fault. The Jeugdstorm leader had told them that they had only to think who lived in the most beautiful houses. How had that scum got hold of the money? Probably by extortion and threats.

Was Jonkers really a Jew? If so, Martin was too. But Martin was fair and Jews were dark. At least, he thought they were. Maybe there were exceptions.

He went on staring unseeingly at the collection of rods, floats and lines. Nothing happened, though some people checked their step in front of the closed shop and some spoke to others, their faces stony.

Arnold turned away from the fishing shop and drifted slowly back. At the corner he glanced over his shoulder again.

Then he saw him.

Martin Jonkers came out of the shop door, crossed the road and hurried in the opposite direction.

For a moment Arnold did not know what to do. Then he started to follow him.

It was easier than he had expected. Martin left the street without once looking behind him. He turned left, followed a narrow street along a canal for a time, crossed a bridge and carried on along the other side. They were gradually leaving the center of town and Arnold was running more risk of being seen.

[36]

There were only a few pedestrians, and he would certainly be spotted if Martin looked around.

But he didn't. On the contrary, he seemed to be in still more of a hurry. As they approached their school, he had a lead of nearly a hundred yards, and when he turned off again it took Arnold some time to reach the corner. He found himself in a street that sloped gently down to the harbor. A couple of fishing boats were moored there, and some rowing boats were bobbing up and down by the quay.

There was no sign of Martin.

Arnold's curiosity turned into suspicion. His father must have been right: the Jonkerses were no good. Martin had probably been sent out to do some dirty trick or other; they had not learned their lesson last night.

Arnold walked on toward the quay. It had stopped raining, but a chilly northwesterly wind was blowing in his face. Everywhere looked deserted.

Two houseboats were moored across the water, beyond the loading area of the mill. They were unpainted and badly maintained, with reddish brown strips of rust showing just above the waterline. Frayed curtains hung at the windows of the nearer boat. He watched for a couple of minutes, but nothing happened.

Arnold bit his lip. Martin *must* have noticed something. He was probably sitting somewhere laughing at him, and on Monday morning the game would begin again. Hey, Arnold, was it fun down at the harbor? Didn't you catch a cold?

Just then he saw the houseboat curtains move. His heart started to beat fast. There was someone in the boat. Martin? Or someone else? He peered across the small harbor until his eyes watered.

The wind was blowing more strongly now, and the drafty alleyway offered little protection; after a quarter of an hour he was shivering. After twenty minutes his feet began to hurt. Twice a couple of men walked past, but they took no notice of him.

He was on the verge of going home to think things over when someone suddenly walked down the gangplank leading from the houseboat. It was a big, fair boy, about seventeen years old; he was carrying a shopping bag. He stepped onto the quayside without haste and disappeared up the street down which Arnold had come.

Arnold was fed up. He had been hanging around all this time for nothing. Cursing under his breath, he dug his hands in his pockets and left the alleyway.

That was a mistake. At that very moment Martin Jonkers appeared, also carrying a bag. He looked around before stepping onto the quay.

It took Arnold exactly one second to dive back into the shelter of the alleyway, but still he was not certain if Martin had seen him and he dared not risk looking around the corner. For a full minute he stood motionless, pressed against the brick wall. Then he peered cautiously along the front. Martin Jonkers had disappeared again.

Arnold waited a minute or two, watching the boat, but when nothing else happened he made his way around the quay and approached the boat. It looked securely shut—padlock on the door, thick curtains at the windows facing onto the quay.

He walked up the plank, feeling the slight movement under his feet. The padlock looked sound, but the iron staple on the doorpost was rusty and one of the screws had broken off. After a quick look over his shoulder, Arnold took out his penknife. In a few minutes he had loosened the other three screws and the lock gave way. He put the screws and padlock in his pocket and pulled open the door.

[38]

The interior of the houseboat was even shabbier than the outside. Dust had accumulated on the floor, wallpaper had peeled from the walls, the narrow window ledges were mildewed and the floor cracked under his feet.

But no one was living in the houseboat anymore. It was an indescribable mess: boxes and paper everywhere, a sink filled with bottles and at least twenty bicycle tires thrown carelessly against one wall.

For a while Arnold stood frozen with amazement, oblivious to the risk of being caught. He *knew* these were stolen goods! He pulled aside some sheets of gray paper. There—packets of coffee and tea. Tobacco in another box. And those bottles in the sink were Dutch gin and brandy. Or so the labels said. And bicycle tires! Brand-new ones!

Arnold forgot how cold he had been. He forgot that he was behaving like a common burglar. He knew only that he had discovered something very important. It had all been in the papers, weeks ago: several shops had been robbed. He could not remember exactly which ones, but they must have been grocers' and bicycle shops. He felt the firm rubber of one of the tires. How much would a thing like that cost these days? And here they were for the taking!

He made his way through the boxes and opened a low door to another room. The mess was even worse here. Empty cartons, about ten packages of tea and sheets and towels everywhere. Arnold carefully pulled a pile of sheets to one side. A faint smell of gasoline reached his nostrils. The smell was coming from five cans, packed in a big box.

He carefully replaced the sheets, closed the door and left the boat. He felt a strange excitement and his hands shook as he tightened the screws. The stuff in the houseboat must be worth hundreds of guilders. Maybe even more than a thousand.

All at once he knew what he could do. He left the quayside

and hurried into town. A quarter of an hour later he was in his room.

He took a piece of paper and after a moment's thought wrote in block letters:

> I KNOW WHAT YOU'VE GOT IN THE BOAT, AND I KNOW WHERE IT CAME FROM. IF YOU DON'T WANT ME TO TELL ANYONE ABOUT IT, LEAVE TEN GUILDERS UNDER THE WHITE STONE AT THE ENTRANCE TO THE PARK AT 7 O'CLOCK ON TUESDAY EVENING.

He read the note through twice. When he was certain nobody would recognize the writing as his, he folded the paper. There was an envelope in his desk drawer, and he found a stamp in the dresser downstairs. Then he left for the post office.

He wished he could see Martin's face when he found the note on Monday! It would serve the bastard right, and Arnold would be ten guilders richer; a lot more than the miserable twenty-five cents pocket money he got each week. They'd pay all right. At least—he paused—as long as Martin found the note himself. There was only one way to be sure of that.

In ten minutes Arnold was back at the harbor. It was as quiet as it had been earlier that afternoon. He went up the gangplank, tore open the envelope and shoved the folded note through the gap between door and sill.

Then he sauntered back into town.

CHAPTER SIX ✐

Thursday, May 7, 1942

IT was a light evening: The setting sun shone through a thin bank of cloud, dyeing the houses orange.

For the second time that evening, Arnold cycled past the entrance to the park, to keep a lookout as he had done before. No trace of Martin Jonkers and his friend this time, though. They had been there yesterday evening and the evening before, hiding among the bushes some thirty yards from the white stone. He'd had no difficulty spotting them as he rode past, showing no interest in the white stone.

He turned and rode back again, more slowly this time. He braked suddenly at the white stone, dismounted and examined his bicycle as if there were something wrong with it. Fiddling with the spokes, he took another look around. There was no one to be seen.

He went quickly to the stone and felt in the small hollow beneath. In a moment he had a small box in his hand. He dropped it quickly into his pocket, jumped on his bicycle and made off.

It had taken no more than a few seconds.

Back in his room, he took out the box. The lid was stiff, and his fingers shook as he tried to open it. Then his face jerked in a grin of triumph. There they were, four folded bills—ten guilders! He took the bills out of the box and smoothed them on the table. Ten guilders! More money than he had ever had before. And so easily earned! But he had a right to it—Martin Jonkers had been picking on him so often. They had paid promptly, too, so they were really scared. They might have paid more if he'd asked for it. . . .

Suddenly he felt warm. Ask for more! That was it! In two weeks' time, say. He mustn't rush it—and he must choose another place, of course.

He folded the bills and put them between the back pages of his stamp album. Then he walked downstairs, whistling.

He bumped into his sister in the hall. She looked at him with a mixture of scorn and surprise.

"My, you're cheerful! I haven't seen you like this for ages. Just won a lottery?"

Arnold felt his color rise. His cheerfulness turned into irritation. "Oh, bug off! If I want to whistle, I can whistle, can't I?"

Rita's surprise increased. "I didn't say a thing," she said. "You can whistle for hours for all I care. But you've been going around with a face like an earwig's these past few days, so I'm bound to think it's odd."

"*You* don't have to think anything's odd," Arnold said. "Go out with your boyfriends again tonight, why don't you? You don't mind them whistling after you, do you?"

"That's none of your business," snapped Rita. "If I want to go out at night, I *will!* After all, I can't help it if a snotty kid like you is too young for that kind of thing."

"Oh no? I suppose you think—"

Mrs. Westervoort put her head around the door. "Oh, children, do you have to behave like this? Can't you treat each other normally just for once?"

"I'm perfectly willing to treat normal people normally," Rita said.

"You're always complaining about something," Arnold said.

"I wasn't complaining about anything. But he flares up if you so much as look at him. All I did was ask if he'd won the lottery, and he exploded!"

Mrs. Westervoort sighed. "Is this true, Arnold?"

He looked obstinate. "She's always sticking her nose in."

"Sticking her nose into what?"

"Oh, nothing. Leave me alone." Arnold walked past his mother into the living room, angry with himself now, too. He shouldn't have reacted like that. They might notice something unusual, and that was exactly what he wanted to prevent. The only thing he could do now was distract their attention.

He went over to his father, who was making notes at his desk in the corner. A couple of books lay open in front of him.

"What are you doing?" he asked quickly.

Mr. Westervoort tapped one of the books. "Do you know what this is?"

"No."

"The Civil Code."

Arnold looked at the acres of small print, obviously not written for the reader's entertainment. "Do you have to know all that?"

"Just the most important bits. You can't become a mayor overnight."

"Will it take long?"

"Until I'm mayor? Next year, maybe."

"Will we be moving, too?"

"I expect so." Mr. Westervoort looked at his son. "Why all these questions?"

Arnold thought rapidly. "Well, just—anyway, I'd be going with you, wouldn't I?"

Mr. Westervoort smiled. "That would be most sensible, yes." He ruffled his papers again and then said, "Listen, Arnold, I need a dictionary. Will you get me yours?"

"German dictionary?"

"No, Dutch."

"It's on its way." He went upstairs, two at a time, pleased that his tactics had worked. As long as his mother didn't start moaning again. He could hear her in the kitchen. Rita was in the hall putting on her coat. Dictionary in hand, he waited at the top of the stairs for her to go.

A couple of seconds later the door closed behind her and Arnold heard the tap of her heels fading away. When he went into the living room his mother was looking out of the window.

"I can't control that child anymore," she complained. "She goes her own way, does exactly what she likes. Can't she consider us a bit?"

Mr. Westervoort pushed back his chair. "You mustn't brood so about her," he said. "After all, what did you do in the evenings when you were seventeen?"

"Not sneak off with any Tom, Dick or Harry, that's for sure."

"Does Rita?"

"I don't know. She's always so late coming home. What if she gets into bad company?"

"As far as I know, she's always been with Jürgen."

"And Manfred. . . ."

Mr. Westervoort frowned. "That's what you call bad company?"

"Not exactly, but . . ." she faltered.

"Maybe we should ask the boys to come here more often." A smile came to his lips. "I could practice my German. That wouldn't be such a bad idea." He took a chair and pressed his wife into it. "I have something to tell you both," he said. "Arnold, come over here and sit down."

Arnold sat down. His father seemed really excited.

"I probably won't be able to celebrate my birthday at home," Mr. Westervoort announced.

Mrs. Westervoort looked at her husband blankly. "Aren't you going to be at home on June 20?" she asked.

"No," he said, smiling. "I have to go to an important meeting."

"Oh, another."

"No, not just another. I've had a personal invitation from our Leader."

"What!"

"There's an important rally in Utrecht on June 20, in the soccer stadium. All leading party members have been invited."

"Do you have to go?"

For a moment he looked annoyed by her lack of enthusiasm. Then he said hotly, "I can't miss it, Gea. I *mustn't* miss it! This is the chance of a lifetime. Would our Leader have invited me if he didn't see anything in me? This isn't a rally for all the NSB comrades—the stadium is far too small for that—no, only the ones who have done most for the movement will be there."

"Are you going on your own?"

"No. Goossen, our group leader, is going too." He looked at his wife's grave face. "Aren't you pleased?"

"Me? Oh yes. I'm just sorry about your birthday."

"My birthday is less important. Besides, then we can celebrate two things at once!"

"What are you all going to do at the rally?"

"Well, it's about—how shall I put it?—about the comrades' solidarity with our Leader. It'll be a tremendous demonstration. It will be broadcast, of course, and everyone will be able to hear that we want victory for National Socialism and the salvation of our country and our people. People will have to change their minds about us!"

[45]

Arnold had almost forgotten the argument with his sister. His father and the Leader of the movement, Anton Mussert! And it would be broadcast, too! "Can't I come too, Dad?" he asked eagerly.

Mr. Westervoort laughed. "Afraid not—though I'm glad you asked. Why not send our Leader a card or a letter? He'd be pleased, and you may get a message back. Then you'll know you're part of it!"

Seeing Arnold's disappointed face, his mother nodded. "Do as your father says, son."

Mr. Westervoort put his hand on his son's shoulder. "There are important times coming, Arnold, and we're going to need people of good, sound Germanic stock. Me today, you tomorrow! Remember that."

Arnold felt again the strange tingling that these words produced. He nodded silently.

"Fine." Mr. Westervoort's eyes were filled with emotion and pride. "I'm pleased with you, Arnold!" After a moment he went on in a different tone, "Incidentally, have you had any more trouble from that, er, Jonkers boy?"

Arnold felt his face turning red. "Jonkers?" he stammered. "Martin Jonkers? Er, no. He wasn't at school for a couple of days, that's all."

"So he's stopped bothering you?"

"Yes."

"What about the others?"

"Well . . . no more than usual. Less, in fact."

"Good. I've always said that scum had to be taught a lesson. If they bother you again, you must let me know at once."

Arnold nodded.

CHAPTER SEVEN ✉

ALTHOUGH the history test was not difficult, Arnold could not concentrate. His thoughts kept wandering back to the previous evening. He had hidden the ten guilders carefully, but his mother might find them when she cleaned his room!

Then there was Martin Jonkers. Arnold had been extremely careful yesterday evening, but could he have been spotted from somewhere else, with binoculars, for instance?

Arnold flushed. He stole a glance at his classmates, but they were busy writing. All he could see of Martin Jonkers was his blond head in the far corner of the room.

"Arnold!" Mr. Dijkman's voice was loud and dry.

Arnold was startled. Everyone looked up.

"Stick to your own work, you hear?"

"Yes, sir," he stammered. "I wasn't doing anything—"

"Quiet!" the teacher retorted.

The class started to buzz.

"Silence!" ordered Mr. Dijkman. "Back to work, everyone."

Arnold bent over his paper, conscious of the suppressed

laughter. He would dearly love to teach them all a lesson, he thought. Instead, he had to keep his mouth shut and virtuously answer a whole lot of questions. Fingers clenched around his pen, he jotted down a couple of sentences almost without thinking.

Voices sounded in the corridor, loud footsteps, the slamming of doors, and then a receding murmur. The class stirred for a moment, but soon everyone was hard at work again. Then the noise in the corridor grew louder again, there was a firm knock at the door and the headmaster was standing on the threshold, his face grim. "May I disturb you for a moment, Mr. Dijkman? There are two 'gentlemen' "—he gave the word a special emphasis—"here who would like to check something."

Two men in the uniform of the German police appeared behind the headmaster. The class sat motionless.

His face white, Mr. Dijkman came out awkwardly from behind his desk. "That will be difficult, Mr. Borger. We've just started a test."

The head made a reassuring gesture. "It will only take a few minutes," he said.

Some of Mr. Dijkman's self-confidence returned. "It's a particularly important test," he insisted. "It affects the final marks at the end of the year."

The head nodded understandingly. He turned back to explain to the Germans, but for them the conversation had evidently gone on too long already. Elbowing Mr. Borger aside, they strode into the room and faced the class.

"All empty your bags!" one of them ordered, in very good Dutch. There was total confusion for a moment or two; then two of the students folded their arms. The rest of the class immediately followed suit. Only Arnold bent down to pick up his bag.

The Germans stiffened. "Final warning!" they snapped. "Empty your bags! At once!"

Mr. Dijkman clenched and unclenched his hands. "Please do as you are told," he said hoarsely. "It's no good."

The class obeyed, but not in the way the Germans expected. As if by prior agreement, they picked up their school bags and emptied them on the floor. Books, papers and pencil cases scattered all over the floor. Then the students began to crawl through the mess, delving for their own property and chattering excitedly.

"Silence!" roared the German who had spoken before. "Sit down! All of you, sit down!"

They obeyed sluggishly, loose leaves and papers still fluttering to the ground.

The Germans looked around the classroom, then began to empty all the lockers. Books were shaken out, diaries checked, notebooks thumbed through. In five minutes they had their first find: A drawing fluttered out of Marloes ter Winkel's diary, a drawing of the Führer, Adolf Hitler, crossing the North Sea in a rowing boat. The caption read in German: *"Wir fahren gegen England."* "Where did you get this rubbish?" asked the policeman.

White-faced, Marloes said, "I don't know."

"This is your diary?"

"Yes."

"Then you must know how you came by this."

Marloes's eyelids twitched nervously. "Someone must have hidden it there."

The Germans grinned. "Always the same excuse. Your name?"

"Marloes."

"Marloes what?"

"Ter Winkel."

The room was completely silent. The headmaster and Mr. Dijkman watched, their faces pale, the history test forgotten.

"You haven't heard the last of this!" One of the men made a note of her name and the search continued, though finding the drawing seemed to have satisfied them and they worked less thoroughly. They felt inside Arnold's locker indifferently and only one piece of paper came out, but from three rows away one could see what it was: a primitive but perfectly recognizable drawing of Mussert, the NSB Leader. Printed next to it were the lines:

> I'm only small, but I think I'm big,
> And wherever I go they call me a pig.

A wave of excitement ran through the class.

Arnold struggled for breath. "That isn't mine," he shouted. "They put it in my locker! The bastards! The rotten bastards! They've always got it in for me!"

"Shut up!" barked the German. "Your name?"

"I didn't do it!" he protested again, his eyes burning with tears of rage and shame. "I hate that kind of thing. My father—"

He got no further. The policeman dragged him from his desk, shouting angrily, "Your name—or we'll take you with us!" He released Arnold, who collapsed in his seat.

"Arnold," he whispered. "Arnold Westervoort. But I really—"

"Silence!" the policeman ordered. He turned to the two teachers. "These two will be hearing from us," he said curtly. "We expect you to check on your students regularly. If we find any more things like this"—he waved the confiscated drawings—"we shall not hesitate to take the strongest measures."

Without waiting for an answer, he stomped out of the classroom with his colleague.

[50]

Arnold was stunned. He sat hunched forward, his face in his hands, half listening to the rising commotion behind him. What a foul, rotten, filthy trick! Of course they had sneaked it into his locker while everyone was busy picking up their things. Tears trickled between his fingers and his rage grew until he could not control himself. He jerked around.

"Filthy cowards!" His voice cracked. "Bastards! I'll get you for this! You're always picking on me, always trying to trip me up. But this time—"

Mr. Dijkman went over to Arnold and grabbed him by the shoulder. "That's enough, Arnold!"

Arnold would have pulled away, but something in the teacher's voice prevented him. "It's all their fault," he said hoarsely. "They're always starting—"

Mr. Dijkman's voice was calm again. "Do you think we like what's just happened?" he asked. "Do you think everyone here feels good about it?" He walked slowly back to his desk. "Hand in your test papers."

"I haven't finished yet, sir," said one girl.

"It doesn't matter, Ida. I don't think you're in the right mood to do any more work. I'll just look at what you've done so far."

"But the test counts a lot toward our final marks," a boy said worriedly. "You said so yourself."

Mr. Dijkman looked kindly at him. "Gert, you still have a lot to learn." He collected the work already done and pointed to the untidy piles of books and notebooks. "Now clean up the mess you've made. Properly. You've got till the end of the lesson."

Arnold cycled home that afternoon aware that his classmates had made a fool of him in the most vicious way. Even the German policemen had fallen for it, and he could hardly blame them. It had been an offensive drawing, after all. Should he tell his father about it? He would probably take some action, but

Arnold's life would not be worth living at school. He would have to stick it out somehow.

He put his bike in the alley next to his house and went straight to his room. His stamp album was lying in the same place as yesterday. He opened it and let the money slide through his fingers again. The paper crackled softly.

He might buy stamps with it, he thought. Or a new album. That would still leave some money for stamps, though not for that 1860 series. That cost more than fifteen guilders, so he would have to wait for more money. But why wait? They had paid the ten guilders promptly. He could write another note, demanding at least fifteen guilders, or even twenty. Then he would stop, before it got too dangerous.

He closed the album.

"What have you got there?"

Rita's voice startled him. "What?"

"I didn't know you had that much money."

His hands went clammy. "I saved it," he said weakly.

"Ha! From your pocket money, I suppose!"

"Yes."

"And how much do you get?"

"Er, twenty-five cents a week."

She looked scornfully at him. "Are you trying to tell me you haven't spent a single cent for ten whole weeks?"

Arnold looked straight at his sister. Ten weeks, she'd said. Then she hadn't seen all the money. He said quickly, "Well, I did sell a stamp or two as well."

"Well, well, so you are a dealer now. At least I know who to ask when I need money." She turned, and he heard her heels clicking quickly down the stairs.

For a while Arnold did not move. Then he took the money out of the album, rolled it up and stuffed it in a gap underneath the windowsill.

Sunday, May 10, 1942

The sun was shining brightly and there was a gentle breeze. The streets were full of people, but down by the harbor it was quiet, at least as quiet as the week before. Keeping a wary lookout, Arnold sauntered on to the quay. To be on the safe side, he walked past the houseboat, right to the other side of the factory fence and back again.

It took him nearly ten minutes, but he knew he could put his note in the same spot without being seen. He was asking for twenty guilders this time. It had taken him half a day to find a place where they could leave the money, and he had succeeded in finding an unused shed by the water tower where they could not possibly hide.

He approached the houseboat for the second time, walked up the gangplank and stooped quickly to slide the paper under the door. There was something in the way—the note met some hard object and crumpled up. He smoothed the note out and slid it under in a different place. It stuck again. His fingers shaking now, Arnold tried a third time. No good. They had obviously put something across the door, or even nailed something along the bottom.

Just then he heard the sound of rapid footsteps. He wheeled in a flash, but he was too late. Much too late.

Martin Jonkers and his friend had reached the gangplank, but they were in no hurry now.

CHAPTER EIGHT

THE two boys were blocking the gangplank. The houseboat lay behind him, the water to the right and left.

He had wild thoughts of jumping off the gangplank and swimming away, or shouting loudly to attract attention—but there was no one to be seen on the quayside. All he could do was to rush the two boys.

He lunged forward furiously. But four strong hands caught him and threw him back against the door. The wood cracked.

"You would, wouldn't you, you filthy Nazi," hissed Martin. "But you won't get off so easily this time!"

Arnold's eyes were wide with fear. "Let me go!" he panted. "I've done nothing to you."

Martin's friend grinned. "Oh no? What's this, then?" He snatched Arnold's note from his hand and glanced at it, then stared at Arnold. "Just as I thought—the same filth as before!" His fist shot out.

Arnold was no match for the boy, who was a good three years older. He was grabbed and forced backward.

"Martin—open the door!" The boy's voice was sharp.

Arnold tried to kick him, but his opponent seemed to have fingers of iron. Gasping for breath, he was pushed into the houseboat.

Martin closed the door and his friend let go of Arnold. "Sit down!" he ordered.

Arnold swallowed painfully, the fear rising in his throat. Then suddenly he thought about the thousands of men his father had told him about who were in far greater danger. They were fighting on the Russian front, in the east, advancing in spite of the bullets flying past their ears, in spite of the bombs exploding around them. They were fighting for the Fatherland, and against communism, prepared to sacrifice their lives—heroes, fearing nothing and no one. And here he was, his legs like jelly. He could just hear the Jeugdstorm cadet officer: "Only poor little devils get scared, only gutless boys without any backbone know the meaning of fear. True Germanic boys stand straight, radiating strength, with the light of resolution in their eyes!"

Arnold felt the familiar tingling in his veins. His fear vanished and he faced the others calmly. "You can go to hell," he said. "Let me go." He took a step toward the door.

Arnold did not see where the knife came from, but it suddenly glinted under his eyes. "Don't try anything!" snapped the boy.

Martin was shocked. "Karel, are you crazy? You can't do that!"

"What can't I do?"

"You can't—you know very well what I mean."

Karel's eyes never left his victim. "Oh yes, I know," he said slowly, "but it would be the best thing for this Nazi pig!" He lowered the knife. "Now sit down!" he ordered.

Arnold obeyed. He had no choice. His legs felt as heavy as lead and his hands were trembling. "You'll have to let me go," he said hoarsely.

Karel laughed. "Now our little Nazi isn't barking so loudly. Why don't you think up something else? You're good at dirty tricks, aren't you? Learned them at the Jeugdstorm, I expect." He looked at Martin. "They're sick of all that marching and those silly community events. That's why they're thinking up dirty tricks now!" He slapped Arnold's note on the table. "Tricks like this—just what you'd expect of a Nazi!"

Arnold shook his head. "It's not true," he whispered. "You're lying! It's you who are the bastards and thieves!"

Karel put his hand in his pocket. "My, my," he said, grinning. "The boy's got a big mouth, too. From his father, of course."

Arnold started up, but a kick at his legs knocked him back on the floor. Pain shot through him.

"Don't try that again!" snarled Karel, putting away his knife and facing Arnold. "Tell us, Nazi, who knows you're here?"

Arnold bit his lip. He looked from Karel to Martin, who was standing by helplessly.

"Well, anything to say?"

"I won't tell you," Arnold replied.

"So you have told someone," the other barked.

Arnold shrugged.

"Come on, Arnold," Martin joined in. "Who else knows about this?"

Karel said: "I'll get it out of him another way!" He drew back for another kick.

"Wait!" Arnold wiped his hands on his trousers. "I—I'll tell you," he stammered. "Bert . . ."

[56]

"Bert who?"

"Landman."

"Don't know him. Another member of your traitors' club?"

Arnold was silent.

"Speak up!"

"He's a member of the Jeugdstorm, yes."

"When did you talk to him?"

Arnold thought quickly. There might be a chance of confusing them. "Yesterday afternoon," he answered.

"You're lying."

"No I'm not."

"Then why did you come here on your own?"

"I thought it was better. And besides, er, Bert didn't dare."

"Would you believe it!" Karel jeered. "A Jeugdstorm hero, too!" He turned to Martin. "Do you know this Bert Landman?"

"Never heard of him."

"Then he doesn't exist."

"But I don't know many of the Jeugdstorm lot," said Martin.

"Do you mean that this monster"—he pointed at Arnold—"might be telling the truth?"

"I don't know."

Karel leaned against the doorpost, his grin gone. "Come on, little Nazi, you haven't told your folks, have you?"

"My father and mother know nothing about this," said Arnold.

"Where does this Bert Landman live?"

The question took Arnold by surprise. "What? Oh, er, I don't know."

Karel's eyes narrowed. "You mean you won't tell us?"

Arnold didn't answer.

Karel came away from the doorpost. "Where does he live?"

"On Voor Street," said Arnold unwillingly.

"What number?"

"Thirty-five." He clenched his hands. What if they knew the people who really lived there?

"Thirty-five Voor Street," repeated Karel, and said to Martin: "We'll go and see."

Martin looked anxious. "Do you want to bring him back here too?"

"I don't know yet. We'll see. But first we'll tie up our little Nazi." He took a length of rope out of a box among all the rubbish. "Hands behind your back!" he ordered.

Arnold did not struggle. His wrists were tied together, then his ankles. The hard strands cut into his skin, but he said nothing.

Three minutes later they both left. The padlock on the door clicked shut. Then it was quiet.

They'd fallen for it—but for how long? Voor Street was about a twenty-minute walk away. That meant they'd be back in three-quarters of an hour, knowing that he had lied.

So he had three-quarters of an hour. It wasn't long, but he had to try to get free. He tugged at the ropes, but his hands were numb where the circulation had been cut off, and the bonds on his ankles had been expertly tied. After a short rest he rolled over across the rough coconut matting to the middle of the room. There might be something in the mess that he could use to get himself loose. He pushed boxes aside with his bound feet, but found nothing.

He rested again. What time was it? About five, he supposed. Sunlight filtered through the door. He could see that they had nailed a board to the bottom of it, knowing that he would come back, and he had walked into a trap. Karel was the worst—he

[58]

had a criminal face. He probably wouldn't shrink from doing terrible things. Why else carry a knife?

That thought, and the stuffy atmosphere of the boat, made him sweat again. He worked himself into a sitting position and struggled over to the small sink unit. With his feet he turned the handle of the cupboard. It was an awkward position, and by the time the door was open he was exhausted.

The cupboard was empty.

Arnold turned and sat with his back to the sink. How long had they been gone? A quarter of an hour? Twenty minutes? They would just about have reached Voor Street by now. He gritted his teeth and concentrated on getting up. Then he took short hops to the door, let himself down to the floor and began kicking at the woodwork. It made a lot of noise, but after half a minute he was exhausted. Besides, the tight ropes were chafing his skin.

He took a deep breath. "Help!" he shouted. And again, "Help!" It was meant to be loud, but only a couple of strangled croaks came out.

Again he waited for minutes on end, but nobody came. On a sunny afternoon like this, who would be interested in an old houseboat in a deserted corner of the harbor? They would be back soon—and then? They could never let him go; they were scared that he would tell everything. What if he were to promise to say nothing to anyone? He could give them his word of honor, but he knew they would not believe him, not after the lies he'd told. He must get away, and there were probably no more than ten minutes left.

For the second time he struggled to his feet, hopped back to the sink, dropped to a squatting position and scraped the ropes along a hinge, where they caught repeatedly on a screw, but he had to stop when he cut open the back of his hand. It was useless. He got up dizzily, leaning against the edge of the sink where the bottles of drink still stood untouched. The bottles! Glass—sharp glass!

His tiredness fell away from him. He struggled to the sink, leaned forward and took the neck of a bottle between his teeth. He lifted it, turned aside and dropped it. The bottle bounced on the floor and rolled away without even chipping. He grabbed a second at once, his teeth aching as he hopped across the floor with it. This time he aimed carefully before letting go.

The explosion of breaking glass echoed around the small space. Two quarts of liquid streamed over the floor, accompanied by the prickling smell of alcohol. Arnold wasted no time. Careless of his safety, he dropped among the broken bottles and fumbled for a big, sharp cutting piece of glass. Then he began to saw with care. It was much more difficult than he had expected and precious minutes passed before his hands were free, but he cut his ankles loose in seconds. He felt his sore wrists and winced at the shooting pain in his feet as he hobbled toward the door.

At that moment he heard footsteps on the gangplank. The houseboat rocked slightly. Low voices. They were back!

Arnold shuffled backward, grabbed a full bottle from the sink and stood still, just behind the door.

Someone was fumbling with a key. A voice said, "We should have known he was fooling us. He'll soon know all about it, too!"

The door swung open and Karel appeared in the opening. For a second he stared at the broken glass in disbelief. The next moment it was only his split-second reaction that prevented the descending bottle from striking him on the head. Instead, the weapon struck his shoulder and he stumbled back in pain.

Arnold dropped the bottle, leaped for the door and punched Martin in the chest. Martin nearly fell, but managed to grab Arnold's leg. Arnold stumbled. His hands met the wood of the gangplank and he kicked Martin off, once, twice. Then he was free. He sprang up, reached the quay and ran along the embankment. Behind him he could hear furious shouts, but he did not look back.

CHAPTER NINE ✄

ARNOLD wrenched open the door, tripped over the step and flopped into a chair in the living room. He was home.

Mr. Westervoort was busy at his desk. "Is that the way to behave?" he complained. "You've been doing nothing all afternoon and then you burst in like a lunatic! You must—" He turned and caught sight of Arnold's torn hands. "Now where have you been?"

Arnold could not speak. His shoulders were shaking.

"Speak up—what have you been up to?"

"They—locked me—up."

"Locked you up?" Mr. Westervoort left his desk. "You surely don't mean those boys have been at it again?"

Arnold nodded. "I think—they wanted—to kill me."

"What?"

"In a houseboat. They'd been stealing—"

Mr. Westervoort gripped the back of a chair so hard that his knuckles turned white. "Now just listen to me, Arnold. Stop blubbering and tell me exactly what happened."

Arnold looked at his father. "Where's Mom?" he asked, his voice trembling.

"Mom's gone to church."

"What time is it?"

"What does it matter what time it is! Just tell me where you've been. How did you get those welts on your hands?"

"They tied me up. I had—" He tried to swallow. "Can I— have some water?"

Mr. Westervoort took a deep breath. "You expect me to go get that for you? Stop being so childish."

Arnold left the room and came back with a glass of water. His teeth chattered against the glass when he took a gulp.

Mr. Westervoort looked at him silently and then drew up a chair.

"That's enough now—maybe I was a bit unreasonable, but you came storming into the room like a madman!"

Arnold told him the story in fits and starts. "I just happened to be walking along the harbor. There was a houseboat there. The door was open. I went in to have a look. There was all sorts of stuff lying there, bicycle tires, coffee and so on. Then I thought—they must be stolen goods. I was going to leave when those boys came. The—"

"What boys?"

"Martin and Karel."

"Martin Jonkers again?"

"Yes."

"And who's Karel?"

"A big guy, as strong as—"

"I mean his surname."

"I don't know."

"Is he at your school?"

"No."

"What did they do?"

"Tied me up."

Mr. Westervoort hissed through his teeth. "And you just let them?"

"Karel was much stronger than I, and there were two of them. Besides, he had a knife." Arnold drained his glass, feeling calmer now.

"And then they let you go, I suppose?"

"No, they went off."

"Where to?"

"I don't know. I dropped bottles on the floor and cut through the ropes with the broken glass."

Mr. Westervoort seemed to be grinding his teeth. "Where is this houseboat?"

"In the harbor."

"Had you been there before?"

"Er—no."

"Bicycle tires, you said?"

"Yes, and coffee and towels—and tea and cans of gasoline."

Mr. Westervoort did something Arnold had not heard him do before: He swore, long and hard. Then he stood up. "Come on!" he said shortly.

"Where are we going?"

"To the police! What do you think?"

Arnold looked at his swollen wrists. "What about my hands?"

"A few scratches? That wouldn't worry a real Dutch boy! Anyway, you weren't so fussy last week!"

"Yes, but this really hurts."

Mr. Westervoort started to get angry. "What do you think is more important, moaning about your sore hands or helping me to track down a pack of criminals?"

Arnold got up and trailed after his father, who was already at the front door.

"Will you get a move on?"

[64]

"Yes, I'm coming."

It was difficult to keep up with his father's brisk stride. At every corner, Arnold looked warily in all directions, but there was no sign of Karel and Martin.

A drowsy policeman was on duty at the police station. He frowned when he saw Mr. Westervoort's NSB badge.

"What do you want?"

"I wish to report a robbery."

"A robbery," the man repeated. "Right." He got slowly to his feet, shuffled over to a cabinet and took out an oblong book. He put it down on the table in front of him and began to turn the pages one by one.

Mr. Westervoort clenched his fists. "It's very important," he said. "I think you ought to know—"

The policeman stopped him with a gesture. *"Just* a minute, *if* you please. Not all at once. Let's see . . . ah, here we are—robberies."

"I also wish to report an assault on my son here," said Mr. Westervoort.

The policeman looked annoyed and slammed the book shut. "What have you really come about—robbery or assault?"

"Both," said Mr. Westervoort hurriedly. "You ought to know—"

"One thing at a time, please, sir. *You* ought to know you can't expect miracles from us. You people seem to think we've got nothing else to do. Which do you want to report first, the robbery or the assault?"

"The robbery."

"Right." He opened the book again. "Your name?"

Mr. Westervoort began to flush. "Don't you know me? I've been working at the town hall for years!"

The policeman stared at his visitor, taking his time. "I'm sorry, sir, we can't know everybody. People seem to think—"

"Westervoort!" snapped Arnold's father.

"Right. West-er-voort. There. Address?"

"Seventeen Klinker Street."

"Sev-en-teen Klink-er Street. Date of birth?"

Mr. Westervoort lost control. "Are you going to listen to me? There's been a spate of robberies all over town. I come to give you information and you ask for my date of birth! Do I have to summon the superintendent?"

The policeman looked more alert. "Did you say you could give information about robberies?"

"That's what I said, yes."

"You haven't been robbed yourself?"

"No!"

He closed the book. "Why didn't you say so to start with?"

"I *did!*"

"You came to report a robbery."

"That's what I meant."

"Then please say what you mean." The policeman shuffled back to the cabinet and took out another book. "Did you witness these robberies?"

Mr. Westervoort ground his teeth. "No, but my son here knows where the stolen goods are—bicycle tires, coffee, tobacco and gasoline."

The policeman looked suddenly interested. "Bicycle tires, did you say? How many?"

Arnold replied: "At least twenty."

"And gasoline . . .?"

"A few cans."

"Where is all this?"

"In a houseboat in the harbor."

"How do you know?"

"I've been there. They tied me up."

"Who are 'they'?"

"A couple of boys."

"Do you know them?"

"Yes, Martin Jonkers and someone called Karel."

The policeman's eyes narrowed. "Karel Rot?"

"I don't know."

"Big, heavy build, about seventeen?"

"Yes."

"Karel Rot. Just a minute." He was getting up when the telephone rang. He picked it up. "Police, Burema speaking. Yes. What? Right, we're on our way!" He banged the receiver down on the cradle and stared at his visitors for a moment. "There's a fire," he said shortly. "In the harbor. An old houseboat."

A few minutes later, three policemen were bicycling fast in the direction of the harbor. A fire-engine siren began to howl.

By evening the whole town knew what had happened: Two boys had set fire to a houseboat where they had been keeping stolen goods. They had thrown gasoline over everything, and the boat was completely burned out. There was no trace of the culprits. Both the boys' fathers were arrested and released an hour later: They apparently knew nothing.

Monday, May 11, 1942

The morning was overcast. When Arnold got out of bed he felt as if his muscles had been battered with a hammer. On top of that, he had slept badly; the events of the day before kept running through his head.

He went to the window and opened the curtains. A fine rain was falling, and well-wrapped figures hurried along the glistening street. He got dressed and tramped downstairs. Familiar sounds were coming from the kitchen.

His father was the first to greet him. "Morning, Arnold. Congratulations!"

"Congratulations?"

"Yes, congratulations! It's our Leader's birthday today. Had you forgotten?"

Although it was the custom to congratulate the nearest and dearest of someone who was having a birthday, Arnold had not expected his father's greeting. "Eh? Oh no—thank you. Congratulations to you, too," he replied.

"Thank you." Mr. Westervoort went into the hall and got out the black and red NSB flag. He carried it outside, put the flagstaff in its holder and stood smiling at it for a moment before closing the door. "Pity the weather isn't better."

"The farmers will welcome the rain," said Mrs. Westervoort. "Vegetables are dreadfully expensive. When you can get them. And you have to stand in line for hours."

"Oh, those are mere details," said Mr. Westervoort. "There will be plenty of everything again soon. In fact, I read in the paper only the other day that people throw far too much away. For instance, cauliflower stalks can all be used."

"I read it too," she sighed. "Pity you can't buy cauliflowers, though!"

"Well, I'm sure it applies just as much to other vegetables." He turned to Arnold. "Why aren't you wearing your uniform?"

"My uniform? I never wear it to school."

"On our Leader's birthday you should wear your uniform. Go upstairs and change. And hurry, or you'll be late, too."

Arnold shook his head. "I won't wear it."

"*What* did you say?" Mr. Westervoort put down his knife and fork. "You'll do as I say at once!"

"I *won't* wear the uniform," Arnold repeated. "They'll bully me even more."

"We agreed that you'd tell me the minute you had any trouble. Now go and put your uniform on, at once!"

"Koos," began Mrs. Westervoort, "if the boy—"

[68]

"Gea, will you please leave this to me! Do you think they don't make fun of me, too? Do you think I have an easy time? But I just carry on with my work."

"Yes, but not in uniform," Arnold interrupted him.

Mr. Westervoort pushed back his chair. "You stupid fool! Upstairs, I said. At once!"

Arnold left his bread and butter and ran out of the kitchen and up the stairs. He slammed the door, went over to the window and stood looking out, his jaw set.

At eight o'clock his father called from downstairs, "Are you ready, Arnold?"

"Yes. I'll be down in a minute." At last he saw his father cycle away.

His mother looked at him anxiously when he came down in his usual clothes. "Shouldn't you do as your father says, son?"

"I'm not crazy, Mom."

"Arnold!"

"Dad would think differently if he was bullied the way I am."

"Your father's got enough difficulties as it is."

"Probably." He jammed a slice of bread between his teeth and grabbed his bag. "I'm off, then."

He was late. Even so, there were still a lot of boys and girls in the school yard and Arnold soon saw why. At least a dozen tenth-graders were wearing a yellow six-pointed star pinned to their breast, the star that every Jew had had to wear since the previous week—so that you could at least see what sort of people had been squeezing Europe dry for centuries, his father said. But what was this bunch doing wearing the star? They weren't Jewish! What a nerve!

He passed the group. "Hey, Westervoort, shouldn't you have a star?" one of them shouted. "They only cost five cents!" Arnold slipped into the school without replying. Behind him someone started to sing, "It's somebody's birthday, hooray, hooray, it's somebody's birthday today!"

Nothing happened that morning, except for some whispering from the corner where Martin always sat.

At lunchtime Mr. Westervoort was later than usual. When he came in he stared at his son for a moment and Arnold feared another angry outburst, but his father said nothing.

"Is anything wrong?" asked Mrs. Westervoort.

Mr. Westervoort nodded. "I've had a visit from the police."

"About the robbery?"

"No—about Arnold and an insult to our Leader."

Arnold turned red right around to the back of his ears.

"They all knew about it at the town hall. How, I don't know. I'm deeply, deeply ashamed."

"I—I—" started Arnold.

"I suppose you're going to tell me you had nothing to do with it?"

"No—they put a drawing in my locker."

"Who did?"

"Wish I knew."

"Why didn't you tell me? That's what we agreed, wasn't it?"

"Yes, but—"

"There's no 'but' about it!" his father snapped. "You must do as you're told. Got that?"

"Yes, Dad."

"I have to be able to trust you. I don't believe you would ever insult our Leader, but I wonder if you'd dare to stand up for him if you had to."

Arnold kept his eyes on his plate.

"So I think it would be better if you didn't come to Utrecht on June 20."

"Why should Arnold go to Utrecht?" asked Mrs. Westervoort. "I thought you were going on your own?"

[70]

"I'll tell you now before you hear it from someone else—our local Jeugdstorm division has been invited to take part in the ceremony in Utrecht."

Arnold looked up.

"But, as I say—I think it would be better if Arnold didn't come."

"Why?" asked Arnold cautiously.

"I don't think our Leader would like it if he knew there were boys there who didn't dare wear the Jeugdstorm uniform on his birthday."

Arnold bowed his head. His father was right. He had just been trying to make a point that morning. They would get at him anyway, uniform or no uniform. "I'll put it on after lunch," he said quietly.

"That's a good boy," he heard his father say. "A bit late, though."

CHAPTER TEN ✒

Saturday, June 20, 1942

ARNOLD did go to Utrecht after all. It took all his energy and powers of persuasion, but then he did have nearly six weeks. Cautiously at first, then more boldly, he asked his father to change his mind about letting him go. He went out of his way to please. He helped around the house. He did the shopping. He even wore his Jeugdstorm uniform to school a couple of times. And his father finally gave in.

He was on the bus with his comrades, thoroughly enjoying himself. The weather was beautiful and a fresh breeze blew through the open windows.

Here and there people were waving at the roadside. Not many, but at least there were some. It made him feel warm inside. Besides, for today he was free of the everlasting bullying. He was with his comrades. No double-edged remarks, no whispering, no insults. On the contrary, they sang with all their might. Halfway to Utrecht they had almost gone through the Nazi youth repertoire and their leader warned them to save their breath for the main ceremony.

Three-quarters of an hour later they turned into the large parking lot in front of the stadium. Groups of people stood talking excitedly to each other, while more and more came streaming through the entrance. At the edge of the square, keeping their distance, there were people watching in silence.

Arnold shivered suddenly. That tall, powerful figure over there, half hidden between a couple of bystanders, wasn't that Karel? He peered through the window of the bus, but the sunlight dazzled him.

All these weeks he had heard nothing more from Martin and his friend. The police had not caught them and nothing had been said at school. At least Arnold hadn't heard anything. Could Karel possibly have turned up here? He peered out tensely without seeing him again and his suspicions subsided: Why should Karel be here, after all?

"Come on, Arnold! We're here!"

He turned, startled, to find that most of the others had already left the bus. He caught up with his comrades and together they walked to the stadium.

"Wait here," their leader ordered, and they waited, gazing up at the stone and concrete building, as people crowded past, men in civilian clothes and in uniform.

His father must be somewhere among them. He was probably already inside, since he had left an hour before Arnold. Arnold had given him a beautiful automatic pencil for his birthday. It had cost him five guilders, but he could manage that easily, and his father had been very pleased.

After another quarter of an hour, the Jeugdstormers were allowed in too. Once in, they had to wait again, this time for nearly an hour, but they were still taken by surprise when the great moment came at last.

"Stormers, attention!"

They formed up in rows of three. The drummers and standard-bearers led the way, followed by the trumpeters and horn blowers.

"Forward march!"

The drums rolled, the trumpets rang out and, at a sign from the leader, they started to sing:

Youth of Holland, we acclaim
    Our people's great ideal.
We proudly bear the Stormers' name
    And stand as true as steel!

We're on the march, come, close the ranks!
    Young comrades, courage take!
We're on the march, come, close the ranks,
    We march for Holland's sake!

We offer all the Stormers' greeting
    By mountain, field and sea,
In order, strength and virtue meeting,
    Our Leader now we hail!

Come, Holland's lads, and beat the drum,
    Be eager, fierce for truth,
Advance together, Stormers, come
    And beat the call to youth!

At the end of the song the drums and trumpets fell silent and thunderous applause broke out from the stands.

Arnold stood rigidly to attention. So this was it, he thought, the common bond, the rare comradeship his father said existed only among National Socialists. He could not understand why more people weren't affected by it. Or could what one of their leaders said be true: "Only a few are privileged to see clearly what is alive and growing within people"? Was he one of the privileged few?

[74]

Suddenly there was a breathless silence. Arnold craned his neck. "The Leader!" shouted someone.

There he was, walking slowly down the grand stairs and striding into the stadium! It was the first time Arnold had seen him, and he was smaller than he'd expected. Arnold was momentarily disappointed. The Leader had seemed much taller in his photographs, but his walk was buoyant and resolute.

A moment later he had mounted the flower-decked podium. Then came the mass cheer from thousands of voices: "Heil Mussert, heil Hitler! Heil Mussert, heil Hitler!"

Mussert raised his hand and immediately there was silence. No one stirred. Only the banners and flags, the Dutch red, white and blue and the NSB black and red, curled lazily in the faint breeze.

The Leader began to speak.

It was a short speech, and when Mussert had finished, Arnold enthusiastically raised his right arm with the others: "Heil Mussert, heil Hitler! Heil Mussert, heil Hitler!"

Then came the unforgettable moment when thousands of men stood rigidly to attention in the stadium and took the oath. The Leader spoke first and thousands of voices repeated the words after him: "I pledge to be faithful unto death to the Leader of the National Socialist Movement in the Netherlands, Anton Mussert. So help me God."

Arnold scarcely dared to breathe. Now he understood. He understood why they had come from all over the country, and he understood the tremendous ideal for which they must be prepared to sacrifice everything: to pledge their faith to the Leader, to one man who would sacrifice his life for the Fatherland. He had just read in the *Stormmeeuw,* the Jeugdstorm newspaper: "Had Mussert not arisen in the Netherlands, the struggles of our forefathers would have been in vain."

He was startled when the others began to sing, but joined in with all his heart.

> True to the Leader
>   In need and sorrow,
> True to the Leader
>   When storm winds rage.
> True to the Leader,
>   We of tomorrow,
> True to the Leader,
>   From age to age!

Then Mussert spoke again. "I have accepted your oath," he said, "and by accepting the oath I have pledged my faith to you—faith in the principles of the movement, faith in the source, faith in the Fatherland; faith in Germanic solidarity; faith in the league of Germanic states, vital to the future of Europe and her people; faith in the German Führer, who has been called by God to protect Europe from conquest and enslavement, from godless communism and ruthless capitalism. This is my pledge, so help me God, from Whom alone come the power and the understanding to follow our calling, to Whom alone we are answerable for all our deeds, to the end of our days. Heil Hitler!"

An hour later they were back in the bus, singing themselves hoarse. When Arnold went home he could scarcely speak.

Mrs. Westervoort was waiting for him. "How did it go?"

"Fantastic!" he whispered.

"You've got no voice left, my boy!"

"Because of all the singing, Mom."

Rita came in. "Shouting, you mean."

"You can't get over not being allowed to come! Isn't Dad back?"

"No. Didn't you see him?"

"No, not at all, but I couldn't have. There were at least ten thousand people there."

"Exaggerating again, no doubt," said Rita.

"No, really I'm not. The stadium was packed."

"A letter came for you this morning," said Mrs. Westervoort.

"Who from?"

"I don't know. There's no address on the envelope. I put it in your room."

"Didn't you read it?"

She said, smiling, "That wouldn't be right, would it—opening other people's letters!"

Arnold ran upstairs, tore open the envelope and read the note. It was short and unsigned. He felt as if a cold hand were slowly choking him. "You betrayed us, you dirty Nazi," he read. "We will never forget, and we will make you pay for your foul treachery."

His legs turned to jelly. The room spun around. Dazed, he fell on his bed, staring at the note. From Martin Jonkers and Karel Rot—who else? So they were lying in wait—waiting for the right moment to grab him. And he was helpless. He could do nothing.

"Arnold!" his mother called. "Where are you?"

He scarcely heard her.

"Arnold!"

He jumped. "Coming." He walked mechanically downstairs, carrying the note.

"What does it say? May I read it?" She broke off. "What's the matter? Don't you feel well?"

He gave his mother the note. "Here."

She read it and turned paler than her son. "This—this is terrible. How dare they!"

"What's up?" Rita asked inquisitively.

"A threatening letter. They're threatening Arnold because he found out about them—the thefts, you know."

"Oh." She stared at her brother, obviously shocked. Then she said, "You'd have done better not to get involved! You're always sticking your nose in everywhere. Now perhaps you can see how dangerous it is."

"Be quiet, Rita," said Mrs. Westervoort. "Arnold couldn't help it. It might just as easily have happened to you." She laid the note on the table. "We'll wait for Father. He'll know what to do." She shook her head. "Oh, my poor boy, why do things like this always have to happen to you, and after such a fine day, too!"

Half an hour later, Mr. Westervoort came home. He was in high spirits, but that soon changed when they told him about the note.

"The bastards!" he muttered, examining the letter carefully. "Where did it come from?"

"It doesn't say."

"I mean, where was it mailed? Where did you put the envelope?"

"Upstairs." Arnold fetched it and gave it to his father.

"Utrecht," he said. "Look at the postmark. It was mailed in Utrecht."

"Then it *was* Karel," said Arnold.

"What do you mean?"

"I saw him in Utrecht. He was standing watching at the stadium this morning. At least, I thought it was him."

"I shall have to bring the police in again," Mr. Westervoort said, "and if that doesn't do any good, I'll warn our comrades in Utrecht. It's too crazy for words that someone should get a threatening letter for reporting a pack of thieves!"

———

[78]

Nothing happened for weeks. No new notes, no threats—and no news that the police had arrested the two boys. The Utrecht comrades whose help Mr. Westervoort had enlisted said it would be hopeless looking for boys like that. Mr. Westervoort understood. "Our comrades have better things to do, of course," he said. "They can't get involved in everything. We just have to be extra careful."

Arnold *was* careful. At first he hardly dared go out in the street, and when he went to school he behaved like a timid, hunted animal. After all, Martin and Karel might appear at any moment. Or perhaps they wouldn't dare? The uncertainty made him nervous, and that didn't improve his schoolwork. His last tests of the year were poor. The teachers said nothing, but the class was delighted, particularly when he got only two out of ten for German. When the term was over, he flung his bag into the corner. "That's the last of that rubbish for a while!"

Mrs. Westervoort shook her head. "Don't say that, Arnold. Be glad you have the chance to go on learning. Look at your father. He never had the chance to stay at school and study, and you know he has to work for hours every night trying to catch up on what he's missed."

"So what? What good does it do him? I can't see him being made mayor!"

"Arnold, you must not talk like that! Whatever has got into you?"

"Nothing. But Dad's either working himself into the ground—and we're not allowed to open our mouths—or else he has to go to some meeting or other."

"You know how important his work is to him."

"To him, yes, but I'm sick of sitting around keeping quiet night after night."

"Would you like to get out of town for a day or two?"

Mr. Westervoort came in just then. "He's always got the

Jeugdstorm, hasn't he? Aren't they going off somewhere for a week?"

"Not until the middle of August," Arnold said.

"Then you'll just have to wait. Perhaps we could go fishing on Saturday afternoon. If you'd like to, that is."

Arnold cheered up a bit. "Don't you have to go to a meeting?"

"No."

"Can we go to the Bramerdiep, then?"

"Fine by me."

That summer Mr. Westervoort went fishing twice with Arnold. The rest of the time Arnold spent on odd jobs, shopping, reading and feeling bored.

CHAPTER ELEVEN ✒

Tuesday, September 1, 1942

THE first day of school Arnold left home rather late so he wouldn't have to wait around before the bell went. He had timed it well and was able to walk straight in. The porter had written the new timetable up in the corridor. His class was in room 10.

Arnold went to his usual place on the left, but two boys were already there. He saw at once that they had been held back from the year above and were repeating the grade.

"That's my place," he said.

"Was," said one of the boys. "It's our place now."

"I sat there last year."

"Then it's time you had a change." He grinned broadly. "Besides, first come, first served."

As Arnold went to the desk behind, both boys turned and nodded benevolently at him. "Well done, that's right. Kids like you should know their place."

The class filled up. No one came to sit next to Arnold.

Just like last year, he thought. They either bullied him or ignored him completely. He looked around the room. The same faces as before, in basically the same places—except in one desk at the back: a new pupil. Rather sturdy, a thin, sunburned face, light blue eyes and blond hair combed straight back.

Mr. Moolenaar, the geography teacher, came in at that moment.

*"Morn*ing, everyone!"

They shot to their feet.

"Good vacation?" Mr. Moolenaar rattled on. "I assume so, insofar as one can talk about a good vacation nowadays. To begin with—I see a new face and"—he bowed to the two in front of Arnold—"a couple of old faces." He looked at his papers and then addressed the boy at the back. "You're Piet Bergman?"

"Yes, sir."

"Haven't lived here long, have you?"

"We moved here last week, sir."

"Quite. From Hilversum, I see."

"Yes, sir."

"Quite, quite—good, good. Well, I hope you'll like it here."

Arnold looked back over his shoulder. Bergman—he'd heard the name before, but where? It bothered him throughout the Bible reading and prayer, but he couldn't remember.

"We're going to look at the Netherlands this year," Mr. Moolenaar said. "Open your books." Gesturing enthusiastically, he began to explain the origins of the Netherlands. "Sand, gravel and clay," he said. "That's where we live and what we live on."

"Rather him than me," whispered someone.

"How did all this come about? Through the great rivers, the Rhine, the Maas and the Scheldt. Particularly the Rhine, bringing sand and clay from Switzerland and Germany." His voice suddenly sharpened. "Some people even claim that the Netherlands ought to belong to the country it got its silt from. I don't, of course, need to tell you that a low mark awaits anyone who dares to write that down on a test."

"Sir—"

Everyone looked up. Piet Bergman, the new pupil, had his hand up.

"Yes, Piet?"

"Do you give a bad mark if someone expresses a different opinion from your own in a test?"

The class were as quiet as mice.

Mr. Moolenaar cleared his throat. "That depends—"

"I don't think you can do that."

"I don't think it's for students to tell me what I may or may not do, not even students from Hilversum!" said Mr. Moolenaar.

Piet Bergman looked straight at the teacher without speaking, then bent over his book again.

The class breathed again.

Mr. Moolenaar continued with the lesson, but he seemed to have lost some of his confidence. His enthusiasm returned only when he reached the Ice Age. Arnold was only half listening. Why had Piet Bergman said that? Was it something to do with the remark about the test? He looked around and saw the new boy making notes. What a nerve! Arnold could never have said such a thing. His interest in Piet Bergman changed to admiration.

Streaming rain and crackling thunder kept them in the classroom during recess, and the room quickly degenerated into a riot. Someone overturned his neighbor's bag, the eraser thudded against the wall and paper pellets flew around the room.

"Hey, here's a good one," roared Hans van Beek. "Listen!

"Helter-skelter, helter-skelter,
Hitler's hanging in the cellar
With a rope around his neck
And his nasty tongue in check—
Isn't he an awful wreck!"

Cheers broke out. Amidst the noise, Arnold saw Piet Bergman suddenly get up from his desk, walk over to Hans van Beek, snatch the paper from him and take it to the waste-paper basket. There he tore it up, slowly and deliberately. The scraps fluttered from his fingers.

Hans van Beek was too amazed to react, and only when Piet Bergman was back in his seat did one of the two boys who were repeating the grade begin: "Hey, bighead, what's it got to do with you? We don't have to take that, you know!" He got up from his desk.

Piet Bergman's face turned a dull red. "And I don't have to take an insult to the Führer either!" he snarled back.

There was nothing friendly about the silence that followed. The boy sitting in front of Arnold looked glassily at Piet and went slowly back to his seat. Arnold did not move. Piet Bergman—an NSBer too? Almost certainly! At last a comrade at school, and in the same class, too. What's more, one who wasn't afraid!

"How was school?" Mrs. Westervoort's voice betrayed a mixture of worry and interest.

"All right."

"Thank goodness for that. Nothing special to tell us?"

"There's a new student."

"How exciting!" Rita commented sarcastically.

"Boy or girl?" asked Mrs. Westervoort.

"Boy, of course," said Rita quickly. "He's not interested in girls yet."

"Be quiet for a minute, Rita."

"His name's Piet Bergman," said Arnold.

Mr. Westervoort came out from behind his paper. "Bergman, did you say?"

"Yes."

"From Hilversum?"

"Yes. How did you know? Do you know him?"

"Not the boy, but I know his father. Since yesterday."

"Hey, Dad, is he in our movement?"

"Yes."

"Where did you meet him?"

"At the town hall."

"Does he work there?"

"Yes. And now stop badgering me. I want to eat. Gea, is the food ready?"

"Almost."

"There's no harm in asking, is there?" said Arnold.

"No, of course not. It's just that for a month now I've heard nothing but Bergman, Bergman, Bergman."

"But you said you only met him yesterday."

"He's been made town clerk," mumbled Mr. Westervoort. "They appointed him last month."

Mrs. Westervoort said carefully, "Your father had applied, too."

"You applied to be town clerk? I thought you wanted to be a mayor."

Mr. Westervoort tried to smile. "You've more chance of becoming mayor somewhere if you've been a town clerk first."

"That Piet Bergman isn't afraid," Arnold started off again. "He was rude to Moolenaar."

"Was he. Why?"

"Moolenaar said some people thought the Netherlands belonged to Germany because the big rivers come from there—or something like that."

Mr. Westervoort frowned. "Well, well. Did he say that?"

"Yes, and if we wrote it down we'd get a bad mark."

"He can't do that."

"That's what Piet Bergman said, too. And it looked as if Moolenaar was angry about it."

"That Moolenaar will have to watch out," said Mr. Westervoort. "I've already heard things about him that are not too nice."

"He's a good teacher," said Arnold.

"Then he's all the more dangerous, Arnold. I want you to report this kind of thing to me the minute it happens."

"Why?"

"These teachers think they can say anything—and all the time they're undermining authority. There has to be an end to it, once and for all."

"Are you really going to do it this time, Koos?" said Mrs. Westervoort. "I'm so worried that it will affect Arnold."

"No one needs to know what Arnold has just told me."

"What Moolenaar said was true, though, wasn't it?" asked Arnold. "The Netherlands will stay independent, won't they?"

"Yes, of course. But why on earth bring the Germans into it? Why doesn't he mention Britain?"

"Britain doesn't border our country," said Arnold.

"That has nothing to do with it," answered Mr. Westervoort crossly. "I bet he never says a bad word about the British, only about the Germans. Am I right?"

"I don't know."

"Pay attention, and if it's true, tell me at once."

———

That afternoon, Arnold left school before Piet Bergman and waited for him at the bicycle shed.

"Hello."

Piet Bergman looked sharply at him. "Hello," he replied curtly, getting his bicycle out of the rack.

"How do you like it here?" asked Arnold.

Piet half closed his eyes.

"I don't think you're in the slightest bit interested."

It was not the kind of answer Arnold had expected. He clenched his fingers. "But I am," he said.

"I can't think why."

"I'm in your class. I'm Arnold Westervoort."

"Well, isn't that nice." Piet wheeled his bicycle out of the shed.

"I'm afraid you don't understand."

"Quite possibly."

"You don't know this school yet."

"Oh, I will, all in good time."

"Listen, are they all as bloody-minded as you at Hilversum?" asked Arnold. "We're not used to that sort of thing here!"

"Then you'll just have to get used to it!" snapped the other boy, throwing his leg over the bar.

A couple of classmates walked off the school grounds. "Birds of a feather . . . !" they chanted.

Piet Bergman stared after the couple for some seconds. When he turned back to Arnold the look in his eyes had changed. "So, you wanted to . . . talk to me?" he asked hesitantly.

"Yes, I did. But I don't feel much like it anymore. 'Bye."

"No, wait a moment. Don't get so steamed up."

"If anyone's getting steamed up, it's you!"

"Yes, of course. Look, I didn't mean it like that."

Arnold's face was stony.

"I think I—I thought, er . . ." Piet faltered.

"What did you think?"

"I thought you wanted to poke fun at me. My father warned me against that, you see. Then when I saw you waiting there . . ."

Arnold nodded. "My father belongs to the NSB," he said. "Yours does too, doesn't he?"

"How did you know?"

"And your father is the town clerk."

"Yes, but—"

"My father works at the town hall, too."

"Oh." Piet fiddled with his bicycle. "Look—"

"Yes?"

"I'm sorry about just now. They told me everyone here was against the NSB."

"At school, too? I'm the only National Socialist in school." Arnold smiled. "Till now, that is."

"The only one? How have you managed?"

"I don't really know myself. Wasn't it the same where you were?"

"No, everyone in my class was NSB." Piet grew more enthusiastic. "They put us together on purpose. If any one of us had trouble, we all came in on his side."

"You can't do that here," said Arnold.

"No, but at least there are two of us now."

They left the school grounds.

"You must be in the Jeugdstorm, too," said Piet, as they walked away.

"Yes, but I don't go very often."

"Why not?"

"Oh, it's so boring really."

"Boring? Then you should have been with us in Hilversum! Haven't you got an assault course here?"

[88]

"No, but we go tracking sometimes. Two weeks ago I went to a camp. Nothing doing. Only singing, games and walks."

"Sounds just like the Boy Scouts!" teased Piet. "Don't you do any wrestling or boxing or anything like that?"

"No, nothing like that."

"We'll have to try to change all that," said Piet briskly.

They were just about to turn the corner when two boys came out from a doorway where they had been hiding—the same two older boys who were repeating the grade.

"Here they come," one of them jeered. "Let's see if their mouths are as big now as they were this morning."

CHAPTER TWELVE ⚑

ARNOLD felt the blood drain from his face. These two were at least a year older than they were. He braced himself for a rapid getaway.

But Piet reacted differently. He had turned white and his hands grasped the handlebars. "What do you want?" he asked.

"Listen to the scum!" one of them said. " 'What do you want?' Not just a big mouth, but stupid, too."

"If you lay a finger on us you mustn't be surprised if something awful happens to you."

"My, my, and he knows how to talk elegantly. We don't like that kind of manners, young fellow."

"I'm warning you!" snarled Piet.

"In the name of the Führer, no doubt."

Piet turned scarlet. "I'll remember that!" he hissed, pushing his bicycle on.

The boys crowded in on them. Piet was grabbed by the arm. Arnold was hit. Right out of the blue, Piet let go of the handlebars and moved with lightning speed. As his bicycle clattered onto the road, his right fist landed hard in his opponent's stomach. Winded, the boy doubled over, but without giving him time to recover Piet caught him under the chin with his left fist. The boy staggered back and supported himself against the wall, his upper lip sticky with blood.

His friend shrank back.

"The same for you?" snarled Piet.

The boy took his friend by the sleeve and pulled him away. "Come on, Bert, the bastard uses tricks!"

Bert glanced at his opponent and stumbled quickly after his friend. Twenty yards farther on, the friend looked around again. "Dirty bastards!" he shouted. "Filthy Nazis!"

Piet hissed between his teeth. "I'll get them now! What are their names?"

Arnold was too flabbergasted to answer right away. He watched as Piet rubbed his knuckles and picked up his bicycle. Then he said: "Bert Veenkamp and, er, what's the other one called, Harm Huisink, I think. Both of them are repeating the grade. I don't really know them yet."

"I won't forget this."

"What are you going to do?"

"Did you think I'd leave it there? I'm not going to be called names."

"But you've already given him quite a beating."

"Not nearly enough, or they would have kept their mouths shut."

Arnold said, "I thought you never wanted to fight."

"I didn't say that. Anyway, they started it, so I had to."

"Where did you learn?"

"What?"

"Boxing."

"I just told you. In Hilversum, at the Jeugdstorm."

"Could you teach me?"

"Of course. All the other Jeugdstormers, too."

They walked on. Arnold was excited: He had a friend, and not just any old friend but someone with guts, who could box! Two blows and Bert Veenkamp was finished! He said, "Do you want to come to my place for a while?"

"Well, not now. Another time. I have to do my homework."

"Homework? We haven't got very much."

"No, but I'd still rather do it first. My father insists. I'll see you tomorrow, though."

"Yes, all right."

Piet sat on his bicycle and cycled away. "See you tomorrow!" he called.

Arnold's mother had obviously been waiting for him.

"What made you so late?"

"I was talking to Piet Bergman," he said, "and we had a fight."

"Again? Had a fight—with Piet Bergman?"

"No, of course not! A couple of idiots who are repeating the grade. They sit right in front of me. They were waiting for us just outside the school."

"Were you with Piet Bergman?"

"Yes, Mom." His eyes began to shine. "He knocked one of them out. In two blows!"

Mrs. Westervoort shook her head.

"Why must you always get involved with troublemakers? Now this Piet Bergman, too—"

"They started it, Mom. And Piet's fantastic! You should have seen him! He's in the Jeugdstorm, too. He wants to teach us boxing and wrestling. They do that in Hilversum."

"Just what we've all been waiting for," Rita said. "I shall expect you to be my protector from now on."

"It's *true,* Rita."

"Piet sounds like a real show-off."

"That's not true!" Arnold blew up. "If he hadn't been there

this afternoon—you should just have seen those bastards running away."

"Arnold!"

"Those creeps, I mean."

"I'll come and watch your first boxing match," Rita promised.

Mrs. Westervoort looked worried. "Boxing—I don't think you should."

"It's a sport, Mom!"

"A sport? You might be killed!"

Next morning, during second period, there was a knock at the classroom door. It was the porter.

"Good morning, sir. The headmaster wants to see Bert Veenkamp and Harm Huisink."

The teacher frowned. "Now?"

"Yes, sir. Apparently it's urgent."

Arnold's face turned red. He peered slyly at Piet, who seemed to be studying his French grammar quite calmly.

The teacher shrugged. "Bert, Harm—you heard. Been up to something again, I suppose?"

Looking indignant, the two boys left the room.

It was almost half an hour before they came back, their faces pale and frightened.

"Well, boys, that took some time. By the looks of you, it wasn't much fun."

They shook their heads and slid back into their seats without a word.

Arnold only heard at lunchtime what had happened.

He was on the stairs when he heard a couple of classmates talking softly around the corner.

"The headmaster had goons with him this morning. Veenkamp and Huisink got it."

"Why?"

"They'd called those Nazis, Westervoort and Bergman, names."

"So?"

"They reported it."

"The bastards! Let's get them."

"Are you crazy? Bergman will report it. Apparently his dad's got an important job at the town hall. And he can fight, too. He knocked Bert Veenkamp out, and he only hit him twice."

Arnold went on down the stairs. He had heard all he needed to.

"But if all of us . . ." They fell silent as they saw him.

Arnold walked past. He could feel their eyes boring into his back, but for the first time he could feel their fear, too. It gave him a triumphant surge of power.

That afternoon he caught up with Piet again in the school yard. "They're scared," he said.

"I told you, didn't I? You mustn't let them walk over you. You must make them crawl instead."

Arnold looked inquiringly at Piet. "What do you mean?"

"It's what my father always says."

"Oh."

"And my friend, too. He's in the SS. Been there for six months now. He'll be going to Russia soon to fight the Bolsheviks. I'm joining the SS in a couple of years."

"Oh. Hey, I heard some boys say that they were going to get us."

"They wouldn't dare."

"Are you sure?"

" 'Course. They get the jitters when they see me now."

Piet Bergman seemed to be right. Wherever he and Arnold appeared, conversations stopped and groups broke up. They were shunned more than ever.

[94]

The teachers had taken notice, too. They were more careful in what they said—except for Mr. Moolenaar.

"We had a democracy in the Netherlands," he said one day, "just like the Greeks. You will, of course, have learned in history that a bunch of barbarians from the east led by some dictator or other tried to stifle that democracy. Just like the Netherlands, I'd say. . . ."

Two days later Mr. Moolenaar was arrested during recess by the German police. They could not have chosen a worse moment. The whole school was there to see them push him into the Black Maria and drive him away.

Indignant shouting broke out. When the bell rang a little later for the end of recess no one except Piet and Arnold made a move to go inside. Arnold could actually feel the hatred of the three hundred students. He began to sweat.

"They're not going in," he said.

"That's up to them," answered Piet. "*We* are!"

They went to their classroom, but they were the only ones. Even the teacher did not come. Suddenly the "Wilhelmus," the national anthem, sounded outside, sung with an enthusiasm that Arnold had never heard before. Yet to him it sounded more menacing than beautiful.

The headmaster appeared in the doorway, glanced inside and then hurried along the corridor and down the stairs.

It grew quiet outside, but Arnold did not dare to look out. He heard snatches of the head's talk to the students: "I understand. We all understand. You've made your protest, but now . . . gone on long enough. . . . no point in staying outside any longer. It would only . . . and I don't think you would want that. You did the right . . . Go in again and resume your lessons."

They did as they were asked. But there was none of the usual racket. A grim silence prevailed in corridors and stairs, coupled with the almost threatening shuffle of hundreds of feet.

Arnold heard his classmates coming, but he had a book in front of him and did not look up. His toes were clenched in his shoes and he felt very cold.

The class filled up, and still no one said a word. No one seemed to be moving, either. The French teacher sat down behind his desk, started the lesson, dictated, asked questions, but still no one reacted.

Arnold glanced around quickly, long enough to establish that at least three cold pairs of eyes were staring at him. He nervously turned the pages of his textbook and made useless notes, cursing Piet Bergman the whole time. It must have been Piet who had repeated what Moolenaar had said, and it hadn't been so terrible, after all.

That horrible silence—it was ten times worse than anything that had happened before. His hands were clammy and he had to fight the impulse to run screaming from the class. Tears burned in his eyes. The teacher did not know what to do, either. For some minutes he tried to interest his pupils in the lesson again, but finally he gave up and there was only the cruel and relentless silence.

A quarter of an hour had never lasted so long.

Arnold was dreading the lunch break more than ever. What would they do? Lie in wait for Piet and him? Very likely. He had better stay in the classroom until everyone had left. He stayed there, alone. Piet left with the others. Arnold waited, a quarter of an hour, twenty minutes. He looked out of the window from time to time, until he was sure there was no one left in the yard. Then he picked up his bag and left the classroom.

In the corridor he nearly bumped into one of the girls from his class, Marloes ter Winkel. It was impossible to avoid her withering look. "I didn't . . . say anything," he stammered.

She didn't answer. She just moved aside for a moment to let

him pass, as if he were some repulsive creature she could not bear to touch.

Arnold ran out of school, looking to right and left. Nobody to be seen. He hurried home.

"You never get home on time," his mother said. "We started lunch a long time ago."

"I'm not going back to school this afternoon," he blurted out. His voice was raw.

"You're not starting all that again?" asked Mr. Westervoort. "What's up this time?"

"They came for Moolenaar. And now everyone thinks—"

"Who's *they?*"

"The Germans. They took him away in a car. Everyone stayed outside in recess. Only Piet and I were inside. They sang the national anthem."

"What's that you say? The 'Wilhelmus'? The nerve of it! Have they gone crazy? Anyway, why was this Moolenaar arrested?"

"He said something about the Germans. At least, that's who he meant."

"This is the first I've heard of it! Why didn't you tell me?"

"Oh, I didn't think it was too bad, but I think Piet reported it."

"Don't you know for sure?"

"No, he didn't say anything."

"What exactly did Moolenaar say?"

"He was talking about the barbarians from the east. I can't remember exactly what he said. They wanted to destroy democracy in Greece, just like the Netherlands."

"And you didn't think that was too bad? Do you realize what times we're living in? And how dangerous someone like Moolenaar can be? You should be ashamed of yourself! At least the

Bergman boy understood!" Mr. Westervoort took a deep breath. "And you'll go to school as usual this afternoon."

"I'm not going, Dad! They all think I told on him, too."

"Which is indeed what you should have done."

"Why should I ask for more filth to be slung at me?"

"If you don't report these things, you're no better than a coward!"

"How cheerful we are," said Rita. "I'm going to my room."

"You two still don't realize what is going on in the Netherlands. Don't you understand that our society is at stake? And that there are people, especially in education, who are trying to undermine that society?" Mr. Westervoort clenched his fists. "There is only one way to save our Fatherland: unquestioned obedience to our Leader!"

"Before the war—" Rita began.

"*What*—before the war? Are you going to say things were better before the war? How often do I have to tell you: Before the war, the Netherlands was governed by a pack of money-mad civil servants. And that's what they call democracy! Ministers fighting for position, one cabinet after another. And a parliament with a bunch of quarreling scoundrels who could do nothing but spend our tax money. Going on about the most pointless things—they could do that all right! And where did this so-called democracy get us? Nowhere. Half a million unemployed. Poverty. Hunger in thousands of homes, not to speak of street brawls and agitation. Now at last when we've got strong leadership, when you can walk down the street again at night without being afraid of hooligans, now a teacher like this quite deliberately talks about barbarians who help to destroy democracy! I'll say it again: This Piet Bergman did an excellent job. You should follow his example."

"Have you finished, Dad?" asked Rita.

Mr. Westervoort didn't answer.

[98]

"I only wanted to say that at least mealtimes were more fun before the war. I'm leaving!" She was out of the kitchen before Mr. Westervoort could protest.

Half an hour later, Arnold left for school. But he came back when he was sure his father had left for the town hall.

"You won't tell Dad, will you?" he asked.

Mrs. Westervoort shook her head.

When Mr. Moolenaar came back after about two weeks he was paler, and thinner too, as if he had had a bad bout of flu, but as he thanked the cheering class it was obvious that his ironic spirit was unchanged.

CHAPTER THIRTEEN 🖋

Friday, October 23, 1942

IT was nearly six o'clock. Mrs. Westervoort, Rita and Arnold were at the table.

"Didn't Dad say what time he'd be home?" asked Arnold.

"No, not exactly. He said it might well be seven or eight before he was back."

"When does the exam finish?"

"I don't know."

"What happens if Dad doesn't pass?" said Arnold.

"He won't be made a mayor," said Rita.

"He'll pass," said Mrs. Westervoort. "He's worked hard for it."

"Not everyone who works hard passes," said Rita.

"You just work a bit harder for your secretarial diploma! You might get a decent job then."

"I've got a good job," Rita spluttered.

"But you can't spend the rest of your life sitting behind a typewriter, can you?"

"What do you think secretaries do all day?"

"A secretary earns more."

"That's true. But you have to work harder, too, and I don't feel like doing that."

"If you want to get on, you have to get diplomas."

"I don't need to get on. I like what I'm doing, as long as no one bothers me."

"What do you mean by that?"

"You know very well what I mean—Dad and his moods!"

"Rita, I forbid you to talk about your father like that! You get more insolent every day. I wish you'd show more respect."

Mr. Westervoort put his key in the door at a quarter past seven. The three in the kitchen scarcely dared to move a muscle. The kitchen door swung open.

"Well . . . ?"

"Passed!" Mr. Westervoort was beaming. "I passed! First time!"

"Oh, Koos, congratulations!" Mrs. Westervoort hugged her husband. "I'm so pleased. We were so nervous."

"Me too. My, my, what a day."

"Was it difficult, Dad?" Arnold asked eagerly.

"It certainly wasn't easy, son. Quite a lot failed. Sixty of the ninety or so who took the exam."

"Wow! So you were lucky!"

"Lucky? I worked hard for it."

"Well, I meant that as well."

"Doesn't matter, Arnold. Look, I've brought something."

"A bottle of wine! Where did you get that?"

"A place in Utrecht. We've really got something to celebrate now, haven't we?"

That evening the old family coziness was back. They talked and played games and Arnold drank a glass of wine for the first time in his life.

[101]

"Do you know who else I talked to?" said Mr. Westervoort. "Comrade Blokzijl!"

"Max Blokzijl? From the radio station?"

"Yes, him. He told me they need good journalists badly, people ready to commit themselves to our cause. Young men and women of character, courage and conviction. He said the work of the press was exceptionally important."

"That was in the *Stormmeeuw* too," said Arnold.

"Would you like to do that?" asked Mr. Westervoort.

"I don't know, Dad. I've never thought about it."

"What are your compositions like at school?"

"All right. I usually get about 70 percent."

"You'd have to finish school first, of course," went on Mr. Westervoort.

"He's got a bit of time, then." Rita giggled.

"Then you could be trained," Mr. Westervoort continued enthusiastically. "And in the meantime you could start by writing an article for the *Stormmeeuw.*"

"I've never tried that."

"Then it's time you began."

Arnold did. He wrote for a whole week. Pages and pages, about all sorts of things. He studied articles in *Volk en Vaderland* and even rewrote pieces from the *Stormmeeuw.* He did a report on the rally in Utrecht on June 20 and compared it with the article by Van Geelkerken, the Jeugdstorm leader. He was disheartened.

"I can't write like this," he said.

"Like what?"

"Like Chief Stormer van Geelkerken."

Mr. Westervoort smiled. "He's not just anyone, you know. Let's see what you've made of it." He read Arnold's story. " 'We all felt inspired. The flags fluttered proudly in the wind. The three thousand men on the terraces stood stiffly to attention as our Leader entered the stadium. . . .' "

"It's good," Mr. Westervoort said. "You see, you can do it!"

"Then just read what Chief Stormer van Geelkerken wrote."

Mr. Westervoort took the *Stormmeeuw* article.

" 'Our Leader,' " he read, " 'our lives are his! Why? We would not have known the answer at that moment, but an overwhelming emotion, the emotion that never plays one false, filled our hearts with the immeasurable, tempestuous longing to be true to this man, to be true to the limits of surrender within our power.' "

Mr. Westervoort was quiet for a moment. "Well!" he said finally. "But you mustn't compare your writing with this. After all, Comrade van Geelkerken has had years of experience and you're still only fourteen. You'll see, in a couple of years it will be fine."

For two weeks, Arnold went on doing his best to get something good down on paper. At last he succeeded in writing a story that pleased him. He gave it to his father. "Would you like to read this, Dad?"

"Not now, Arnold. I've got to go to a meeting. Tomorrow, perhaps."

"All right."

He put his papers away. But the next day his father was equally short of time. "We're incredibly busy at the town hall," he said. "I have to work late."

The day after that he was visited by the group leader, who did not leave until nearly twelve o'clock.

A week later, Arnold asked again.

"Stop nagging," said Mr. Westervoort. "I'm much too busy."

"It was you who wanted Arnold to start writing," said Rita.

"Yes, but did you imagine I'd have time to look at everything? I said he should keep practicing. *You* read it!"

"I don't know enough about it."

"And I don't have enough time." He put on his coat and left the house.

"Since Dad finished that course he's never at home," said Rita. "He's always going to meetings!"

"I don't like it any more than you do," said Mrs. Westervoort, "but he has to go. He has to know everything that's going on if he's going to be a mayor. If he doesn't, he'll never be appointed."

"So he has to go to meetings to make friends and influence people. Anyway, now that Dad's always away, he won't notice when I'm out in the evenings!"

Thursday, December 17, 1942

Arnold came home whistling. He had every reason to: An 80 percent in math didn't come his way every day. But he stopped whistling as soon as he saw his mother.

She was sitting in a chair by the stove, hunched up like a shivering bird.

"What is it, Mom? Don't you feel well?"

"I'm so cold," she said. "It started this morning. I think I have the flu." She coughed, her face painfully distorted. "Will you fill the stove?"

"But it's stifling in here."

"That's because you've come in from outside." She leaned forward and poked the fire. "The coal scuttle is in the shed."

Arnold nodded, filled the scuttle and lugged it into the room.

"There isn't much left," he said.

"It's the last," she replied. "We'll have to find some peat

[104]

somewhere. Or wood." She shivered. "Will you get me another blanket?"

"Why don't you go to bed?"

"Who'll make dinner if I do?"

"Oh, we'll manage. Anyway, Rita will be home soon."

"I don't like going to bed. It only makes me feel worse."

"But you always make me go to bed when I'm sick."

A fresh burst of coughing took her breath away.

Arnold ran to get the blanket. "Would you like anything else? Something to drink?"

She shook her head. "No—I don't want anything. You go and do your homework."

An hour later, Mrs. Westervoort was no better. Her cheeks were blazing red by the time Rita came home, and her eyes sparkled unnaturally.

"It's hot in here," said Rita. "What are you doing by the stove with a blanket on? You've got a fever. You should be in bed."

"What about dinner?" Mrs. Westervoort feebly protested.

"That'll be all right, Mom. What's the trouble?"

"Caught a cold, I think. A touch of flu."

"Shall I make you a hot lemon drink?"

Mrs. Westervoort smiled weakly. "Lemon? You can't buy those anymore, Rita."

"You must go to bed," Rita said firmly, and Mrs. Westervoort obeyed, climbing the stairs with obvious difficulty. And when she crept between the cool sheets she was shivering all over. Beads of sweat stood out on her forehead.

"Shall I ask the doctor to come?" asked Rita.

"Oh no. Just let me have a good sleep. I haven't had much the last few nights, because of my cough."

Mr. Westervoort came home around six. "Why isn't dinner

on the table? I have to go out again to a meeting at half past seven."

"Mom's sick," said Arnold.

"Mom sick? Where is she?"

Mr. Westervoort hurried up the stairs. His face was grave when he came back. "She's running a high temperature," he said; "103 degrees. We must get the doctor."

"Is it flu?"

"I don't know. It hurts a lot when she coughs."

"I'll go," said Arnold. He put on his coat.

"Ask him to come at once. And be sure to tell him about her fever. Do you need the flashlight?"

"No, I'll find it all right."

"Be careful."

Arnold walked out into the darkness. A soft rain was falling and the streets were glistening faintly, but that was almost all one could see in the darkened city.

Controlling his sense of urgency, Arnold walked quietly down the street and turned left toward the canal. He followed the white line over the bridge—they had painted it in after five people had fallen into the water in the dark. After ten minutes he found the doctor's house.

A German patrol was approaching as he rang the bell.

He didn't have to wait long. The door swung open and a weak light from the hall fell outside.

"Lights off!" a voice snarled.

"Yes, yes, keep calm." And to Arnold: "Come in."

The door slammed behind him. Arnold was standing in a high-ceilinged hall with a marble floor. Brown doors to left and right. Signs with CONSULTING ROOM and WAITING ROOM on them. A faint smell of disinfectant and ether.

"What can I do for you?"

Arnold could scarcely make out the doctor's face by the hall light. "My mother's sick," he said. "Could you come, please?"

"Your mother's sick? What's your name? Oh yes, I know—you're Westervoort's boy, aren't you?"

Arnold nodded.

"What's the matter with your mother?" The doctor didn't sound any friendlier.

"She's got a fever."

"Since when?"

"This afternoon."

"Couldn't you have come earlier?"

"I don't know. It, er . . . it wasn't so bad at first."

"It's probably flu," murmured the doctor. "I'll write you out a prescription. Wait a moment." He opened the door marked CONSULTING ROOM.

"She's got a temperature of 103," said Arnold.

"Quite possibly," replied the doctor. "That's normal with this flu." He went away and returned with a note and a box. "There are some powders here. Your mother must take some tonight. This prescription is for medication. You can get it tomorrow at the pharmacy." He went toward the door.

"Is it for cough medicine?" asked Arnold.

"Cough medicine? What gave you that idea?"

"Oh, I thought—because my mother's coughing so."

The doctor kept his hand on the doorknob. "Has she had it long—the cough?"

"A few days. She couldn't sleep because of it, she said. It hurts her, too."

"Where?"

"I don't know, but I could see it in her face."

After a moment's silence the doctor said, "I'll come this evening after all. And now go quickly. I don't want any more trouble with the light."

———

[107]

Half past seven, and Mr. Westervoort was pacing up and down the room. "Isn't the doctor ever coming? He should have been here half an hour ago. You did make it clear to him, didn't you?"

"Absolutely, Dad."

"And you've given her one of those powders, Rita?"

"Yes."

"Let's hope it works quickly." Mr. Westervoort rubbed his hands together nervously. "Of all the nights for something unexpected to happen."

They looked at him, not understanding.

"I *have* to go to this meeting tonight," he explained. "They're discussing a mayor's job again. I *can't* stay away." He consulted his watch again. "Twenty-five to eight already. I should be there by now! What's keeping the man?"

The doctor arrived twenty minutes later. He and Mr. Westervoort went upstairs.

Arnold and Rita stayed downstairs, listening to the men's muffled voices above them.

"Mom's very sick," said Rita. "For a moment this evening I thought she couldn't even see me."

"Because of the fever?"

"I suppose so."

The doctor didn't stay long. Footsteps on the stairs, then quiet talk in the passage.

"You must not leave her alone," they heard the doctor say. "One must never underestimate pneumonia. Give her two pills now and then two more late this evening."

"Can't you say anything more, Doctor?"

"I can only say that your wife is seriously ill. I may come back later this evening. There's nothing else I can do for you at the moment."

"Shouldn't she be in the hospital?"

"No point. She'd get the same medicine there. Good evening."

Mr. Westervoort came into the room, his face taut and his hands shaking. "Pneumonia," he said softly. "Her temperature's risen above 103. Rita, will you give her two of these pills? You're better at it than I am."

There was another groaning cough from upstairs. All three of them hurried to her bedside.

Mrs. Westervoort's eyes were brilliant. "Haven't you gone yet, Koos?" she whispered. "You had to go to a—meeting, didn't you?"

Mr. Westervoort looked helplessly from his wife to his two children. "I don't know . . ." he began.

"Go on . . . it's all right . . . Rita and Arnold . . . are here. It's so . . . important for you."

"Oh, not all *that* important."

She shut her eyes and shook her head. "Go . . . go . . . for . . . all of us."

Mr. Westervoort took her hot hands in his. "I know what I should do," he said. He stood up and beckoned Arnold and Rita to follow him.

"Are you going, Dad?" asked Arnold.

"Maybe," said Mr. Westervoort vaguely. "But not now—later. I can't desert her."

CHAPTER FOURTEEN ✒

THE next three days were the worst Arnold had ever known. They took turns, or sat together by the sickbed, helplessly watching the desperate struggle against the wasting fever. The doctor came twice a day, but all he could say was, "We have to wait."

They waited—tense, frightened and uncertain, until Sunday afternoon, when Rita suddenly came running downstairs. "Quick! Come!" she shouted. "Mom's getting better! Her fever's broken!"

They flew upstairs.

Mrs. Westervoort was transparently pale, but she was smiling, which she had not done for the last forty-eight hours.

"I've had a . . . good sleep." It was difficult for her to speak.

"Gea . . ." Mr. Westervoort searched for words. "We've been—so afraid."

She nodded. "You didn't—go to that meeting, did you?"

"No."

"You should have gone."

"But I didn't know . . ." he faltered.

"No, of course not." She looked at Arnold. "Have you done your homework for tomorrow?"

"Homework?" Arnold asked, amazed. "Why bring up homework now, for goodness' sake?"

"There, you see?" said Mrs. Westervoort. "No one keeps an eye on you if I'm not there." She tried to prop herself up on her elbows but sank back at once into the pillows. "I'm exhausted," she whispered.

"You must go back to sleep," said Mr. Westervoort. "Are you two coming down with me?" He turned at the door. "Would you like anything to drink?"

"Soon. A cup of tea."

When they were downstairs, Rita said, "Mom must have something to get her strength back quickly. Steak, or eggs."

"I know a farm where you can buy eggs," said Arnold. "I'll go there first thing tomorrow."

"No you won't," said Mr. Westervoort. "That's against regulations, as you well know. Eggs and vegetables must be bought at recognized shops."

"Yes, but we haven't enough coupons," said Rita.

"Then try to exchange some. We still have tobacco coupons, and I don't need those, do I?"

"Who'd want to exchange coupons with us?"

There was a silence. Then Arnold said, "Bergman, perhaps?"

"Bergman doesn't smoke."

"Clothing coupons, then?"

Rita said: "Mom used up all the clothing coupons only last week."

"Shall I go to the farmer, then?" Arnold asked cautiously.

"No, I won't hear of it! I've just told you it's against regulations. I'll make inquiries tomorrow at the town hall. We might be entitled to a sick ration. Anyway, vegetables aren't rationed yet, are they?"

"No."

"Then you can buy some fresh vegetables first thing tomorrow, Rita."

"From where?"

"You must be able to get carrots somewhere. Or kale."

"I'll do my best."

Rita did her best. She stood in line for hours and managed to get hold of some fruit and vegetables, but she couldn't find eggs anywhere.

Mrs. Westervoort recovered quickly. On Christmas Day she was even allowed up for an hour or two.

There wasn't a happy feel to the day, though. The day before, Mr. Westervoort had heard that he shouldn't expect an appointment as mayor for the time being.

"Is it because of that meeting last Thursday?" asked Mrs. Westervoort.

He nodded. "The next day, two men went to Utrecht. They'll probably get positions."

"Maybe you'll have a chance later."

He shrugged. "Who knows."

"You mustn't feel so bad, Koos."

"I don't even know if I can keep my job at the town hall."

"What did you say?"

"It's Bergman. We don't get along very well."

"I didn't know that."

"He thinks he can find someone cheaper to do the work I do."

"But that's silly! It's the work you've always done, isn't it?"

[112]

"I think he wants to put a friend of his in my place." He turned to Arnold. "Are you still going around with the Bergman boy?"

"Sometimes. At school, anyway. And at the Jeugdstorm."

"Hm. But you've never been home with him, have you?"

"No. He's always busy. I've stopped asking him."

"Does he do well at school?"

"Quite."

"Better than you?"

"No. Why do you ask?"

"Bergman's always bragging about his son. To hear him, you'd think Piet was the best in the class."

"That's nonsense. There are about five better than him."

"And no one is as good at sports as he is . . ."

"That's true. He can run, and skate. At least, so he says. He was junior champion or something last year."

"But this Mr. Bergman can't just push you aside, can he?" Mrs. Westervoort returned to the subject.

"I don't know, Gea. But I'm not happy about it. At that meeting, you know, last week, he had the final say, and two others were selected because I wasn't there. It's what I was afraid of."

"But it wasn't your fault!"

"That's what I said, too. They just said . . ."

"What did they say?"

"That I obviously put the interests of the movement second."

"How mean!"

"There's not much I can do about it."

"Come on, Koos, I've never seen you like this before. You mustn't get down in the dumps. You must do something!"

"I don't know what to do."

"Write a letter."

"A letter? To whom?"

"To our Leader. Tell him exactly what happened, and how they're always passing you over. You'll see—it'll help."

Mr. Westervoort wrote the letter. It took a long time, because he didn't want there to be any mistakes or inaccuracies in it. Three days later it was in the mail.

The same day Arnold came downstairs, skates in hand.

Mrs. Westervoort was pottering about in the kitchen. "You're surely not going skating?"

"Yes, Mom. It may thaw tomorrow. Besides, it's still vacation and I've got a chance to go now."

"Are you going alone?"

"Yes, but there are sure to be other people there."

Mrs. Westervoort looked concerned. "The fog hasn't lifted yet," she said. "You might get lost."

"On a piece of ice a couple of hundred yards square? Oh, Mom, don't fuss. Nothing will happen. I went at least twenty times last year."

"It froze much harder last year."

"I've seen lots of others go past already with skates this morning."

"As long as you promise to get off if it begins to crack."

"Cracking ice is healthy ice!" Without waiting for more objections, Arnold quickly put his coat on and went out of the door.

There was hardly a breath of wind. Cold, thick fog hung in the street, blurring all the shapes.

It was about a twenty-minute walk to the flooded land, and when Arnold reached the water meadows beside the river he seemed to enter another world, a tiny world whose only reference points were a couple of crooked pollard willows. A layer of frost half an inch thick lay on branches, posts and barbed wire.

[114]

He could hear voices through the fog—there really were other skaters. He tested the edge of the ice with the heel of his shoe. There were a few small cracks, but nothing more.

He tied on his skates and glided out over the dully gleaming ice. The gray shapes of other skaters loomed up and disappeared. He recognized two boys from his school but made no attempt to join them. He returned in a big sweep to his starting point, took a short rest and set off again.

His skating gathered speed and power. He raced forward, avoiding tufts of grass sticking up through the ice. Suddenly a crack started ahead of him. While he was wondering whether cracking ice really was healthy ice, he realized that he was quite alone.

He turned again, this time moving along the edge of the reeds. He seemed to be skating over a deep pool, because the ice was pitch-black. There were no other skate marks.

Another crack, loud as a whip.

Arnold was suddenly afraid. This ice was not to be trusted at all. He had to get away as quickly as possible, and he must not stop. Above all, he must not stop.

He peered into the fog, trying to spot holes in the ice, although with no wind it would be difficult to see the difference between ice and open water.

He had almost reached the edge of the black ice when the ice gave way—it was like falling in a nightmare.

Arnold lost his balance and fell forward on the thin edge of the ice, which crumbled away rapidly. His hands clawed at the glassy-smooth chunks. He kicked out wildly.

The brutally cold water tugged at him. He tried to swim, but his left leg suddenly wouldn't work anymore. He realized that the point of his skate was caught, probably in a bit of wire or the roots of a rotting tree trunk. The hole had become an icy-cold, deadly abyss.

Arnold screamed, but the fog intercepted the sound and smothered it in a million tiny droplets of moisture.

He went on struggling, caught at a thicker piece of ice and held on tightly, but his movements were already slowing up—the penetrating cold had a paralyzing effect. Gasping, he tried to jerk his left leg up, but the movement nearly pulled him underwater. If only he could loosen his skates, or at least his shoes. He groped under the water, trying to reach the laces on his skates, but he got no farther than his knees. He would have to duck his head underwater. He would also have to let go with his right hand. The icy cold left him no choice. He took a deep breath.

Then he saw the two boys. They were already quite close when they saw him, too. Their skates screeched on the ice as they braked fast.

"Frerk, watch out!" he heard one shout. "Someone's fallen through the ice! There, where it's deep."

The boys moved farther away from the hole.

"Hey! It's Westervoort!"

They were the boys he had seen earlier. They were in their senior year.

"Get away! It's much too dangerous here!" the first one shouted, turning.

"Help!" shouted Arnold.

Frerk hesitated.

"Hurry up!" The other started to skate off. "We'll go through, too, in a minute!"

"We'll get help!" called Frerk. He began to follow his friend.

Terrified, Arnold shouted, "I'm stuck!"

Frerk stopped on the edge of the dark ice. He dropped onto his knees and then onto his stomach and began to wriggle forward to the hole.

[116]

The ice bent under his weight. Water gushed over the edge of the hole. Eighteen inches away from Arnold he stopped.

"Try to grab my hand!" he said. "But calm down, otherwise I'll be in, too."

Arnold reached out, but his leg was anchored in an icy grip. "My skate's stuck," he gasped.

The other boy came back. "Frerk, are you off your head? *Leave* the Nazi!"

"Shut up!" Frerk snapped back. "And get hold of my legs. Quickly! On your stomach!"

Grumbling, the other boy did as he was told. Inch by inch he pushed his friend toward the hole until he could grip Arnold's outstretched hand.

"Now pull!"

Both boys pulled. The points of their skates clawed into the ice.

Arnold struggled to get loose, and the boys started to slide toward the hole.

"Stop! Don't *you* pull!" shouted Frerk. "Just hold on tight!"

Arnold kept dead still. The water was lapping against his lips. His foot was still stuck.

"It's not working!" Frerk unexpectedly let go and wriggled back. "We'll have to do it another way. Your scarf, Alex!" He took off his own, knotted it to his friend's and threw the end to Arnold.

Bracing themselves on the thicker ice beside the hole, they began to pull again.

"We're crazy!" said Alex again. "We'll never make it!"

Arnold could scarcely keep hold of the scarf with his numbed fingers, but the fear that they might abandon him gave him gigantic strength. "Try to pull your foot loose when I say so," ordered Frerk. He made a toehold in the ice. "Now!"

Arnold jerked up his leg. There was a dull, crackling sound—and he was free!

The boys staggered back. Arnold held on tight until he was lying on the edge of the ice. Then he crawled on hands and knees to a safer spot. Water streamed from his clothes. A length of muddy barbed wire trailed after him.

He did his best to scramble to his feet, but when he tried, black spots danced before his eyes.

Frerk bent down, removed the barbed wire from his skate and threw it in the rushes. "Go home!" he said abruptly.

Arnold nodded and a moment later was standing shakily on his feet.

When he skated slowly back, Frerk and Alex had already disappeared in the fog.

CHAPTER FIFTEEN ✍

THE thaw began the same day. Arnold hardly noticed, because it took him hours to get warm again. He had thrown off his clothes the minute he came in and crawled into bed with three hot-water bottles.

His mother said no more than, "Thank God those two boys were there. You must go and thank them tomorrow."

All that was left from Arnold's escapade was a cold, but that, too, had passed in a couple of days.

A week later, under pressure from his mother, Arnold wrote a very short note indeed: "Thank you both for pulling me out of the water. Arnold Westervoort."

Back at school after the Christmas vacation he saw Frerk several times in the school grounds, but Frerk pretended not to see him.

He heard an improvised song coming from a small group he passed: "If only he'd sunk, there'd have been one less skunk. . . ."

His face a furious color, he went to the classroom. So everyone knew!

He looked at Marloes ter Winkel's back as she sat there in

front of him, at the soft line of her shoulders, the dark blond curls that danced on her neck with every movement of her head, and her face with its laughing eyes, whenever she turned sideways. He would have liked to talk to Marloes, but of course he couldn't. Marloes and her friends hardly bothered with the boys in the class. Anyway, he remembered only too well how she had looked at him the day Mr. Moolenaar was arrested.

"Arnold, what are you staring at?" Mr. Dijkman's glance was hard and cool.

Everyone looked at him. Arnold turned bright red. "Me? Nothing, sir," he stammered.

"Then answer my question."

Arnold was silent. The blood rushed to his head as he vainly tried to collect his thoughts.

"What did I ask, Arnold?"

"What—what I was staring at."

The class roared with laughter.

"No, I mean before that."

"I don't know, sir."

"You may choose," said Mr. Dijkman icily. "Either pay attention or leave. I will give you one more chance. Understand?"

"Yes, sir."

Arnold stared fixedly ahead. Why did he always make such a fool of himself?

"Idiot," whispered Piet beside him. "You always let them walk over you."

Arnold pretended he hadn't heard, but he knew that Piet was right. It was perfectly normal not to hear a question once in a while. He shouldn't have reacted so guiltily. Dijkman had been mean, though.

A week later the school building was taken over by the Germans. They were kept busy for two days, carrying seats and desks to a deserted cigar factory on the other side of town. Its entrance gave onto a narrow street where there were other factories.

The factory was chilly and stuffy, and the pervasive smell of tobacco hung everywhere. Boxes filled with sand stood in the "classrooms" and corridors. "What's this for?" someone inquired.

"That's for you to play with during recess," said Johan Laning. "But you have to bring your own little spade."

He turned out to be right. In the very first recess a sand fight broke out and was soon in full swing.

The headmaster intervened at once. "I will not have this," he said. "Lock the boxes! The staff will keep the keys."

For three days the sandboxes—which were there as a fire precaution—were locked. Then the fire department found out and insisted that the locks be removed again.

There was also a change in the timetable. When it was time for German, Mr. Geurtsen, the classics teacher, appeared, much to their astonishment.

"I hope to be teaching you German in the coming months," he explained.

"Is Mr. Bouwman ill?"

"No. The change is purely a matter of internal reorganization."

Arnold wondered if all classics teachers talked like that, but he soon noticed that Geurtsen's lessons were clear and well arranged.

Apart from Mr. Geurtsen, Mr. Dijkman, the history teacher, and Mr. Hoving, the English teacher, also suddenly turned out to be very good at German. Mr. Bouwman, on the other hand, took over a number of history and English lessons.

"Have they been properly trained to teach German?" asked Mr. Westervoort when he heard about it.

"What do you mean?"

"You can't teach German just like that. You have to have a certificate, don't you?"

"I don't know," answered Arnold. "All I know is that Geurtsen is no worse than Bouwman."

"That's not what I'm interested in. I have a feeling something isn't quite right. I think I'll look into it."

Next day Mr. Westervoort came home, saying, "I thought as much! They're trying to get out of it!"

"Out of what?"

"*Arbeitseinsatz*. It's everyone's duty to work for the country in the labor service. If they don't, there will be chaos in a very short time. The work isn't always pleasant, but no one with any sense of responsibility would try to shirk it."

He was silent for a moment and then continued, "What's more, I don't understand the school authorities' allowing it!"

"Allowing what?"

"Haven't you caught on yet?" said Mr. Westervoort snappishly. "German teachers are exempt from the *Arbeitseinsatz*. That's how Hoving, Geurtsen and Dijkman are trying to avoid it. But if I have anything to do with it, we'll soon put a stop to that sort of unpatriotic attitude."

Mr. Westervoort didn't have much success, however, because Mr. Hoving, Mr. Dijkman and Mr. Geurtsen all turned out to be studying for their German teaching diplomas. The fact that the course could take several years made no difference; for the time being, they did not have to take part in the *Arbeitseinsatz*.

That did nothing to lighten Mr. Westervoort's mood. When, to top it all, the news came through on February 2 that the German troops had surrendered to the Russians at Stalingrad, he became even more somber. "It's not going well," he mumbled.

"Can't they see that? The threat from the east, the worst danger of all."

On Friday evening, February 5, Mr. Westervoort came home late from a meeting. He was as white as a sheet. "Have you heard?"

"Heard what?"

"General Seyffardt has been shot."

"What? General Seyffardt of the Volunteers' Legion? Is he dead?"

"I don't know. They said at ten o'clock that his condition was serious. Haven't you heard any reports?"

"We haven't had the radio on."

Mr. Westervoort turned the radio on. "Maybe they'll give us more news at eleven."

They waited tensely. There was music, then the sound of eleven o'clock striking. Then came a man's heavy voice: "The Commandant of the Netherlands Volunteers' Legion, Lieutenant-General Seyffardt, was attacked this evening. He was shot down in cold blood by two men in the hallway of his home. Despite his severe wounds, the general succeeded in telephoning the police and was immediately taken to hospital. NSB secretariat sources report that his condition is critical and there are fears for his life. There is no trace of the gunmen."

Mrs. Westervoort looked at her husband, her eyes wide. "How terrible! Whoever could have done such a thing?"

"Terrorists, of course! From the so-called resistance."

"But, why?"

"Why—why! Do you need to ask? Don't you know that our movement is now the only legal one, and that our Leader is to become prime minister? Many people in the Netherlands must be bursting with hatred and jealousy! Given half a chance, they'd murder him—but our Leader has a bodyguard. That's why the gunmen picked another victim." Mr. Westervoort clenched his fists. "The blackguards! If they catch them—!"

Next day General Seyffardt died, and Mr. Westervoort suddenly had no spare time at all.

He even had to work late at the town hall on Monday evening, but what he was doing there they did not know.

Tuesday, February 9, 1943

It happened soon after the beginning of the third period. The street where the cigar factory stood was suddenly full of noise: the throbbing of motorbikes, the slamming of doors, shouted commands.

The class was immediately uneasy. Mr. Geurtsen walked to the small window and looked down. His face was set as he turned back. "A raid," he said. "Stay in your seats."

The Germans pushed their way into the building. Footsteps tramped up the stairs. The door was jerked open. A German soldier stood in the doorway.

"Which class?" He was pointing a sten gun. A man in civilian clothing appeared behind him.

Mr. Geurtsen said calmly, "This is the tenth grade. What do you want?"

"Continue!" The German left, the door slammed, the class sat petrified. Why were the Germans here? For the teachers? Unlikely, or they would not have left Mr. Geurtsen alone.

They soon knew the answer. Mr. Geurtsen had lost control of the class, who crowded at the windows watching the abrupt movements of the soldiers in their gray uniforms. "It's some of the juniors and seniors," Johan Laning said suddenly. "They're taking them away."

Arnold was standing behind the others. Over their shoulders he caught a glimpse of what was going on in the street below.

Ten or twelve boys were being herded into the waiting police vans. Frerk was among them, Frerk Wiersema who had pulled him out of the water. What could he have done to make them take him away? And the others? Had they been working for the resistance? Or were they being rounded up to work for the Germans? If so, why only these, and not all the boys from the eleventh and twelfth grades?

The van doors closed and the Germans raced away.

Mr. Geurtsen said quietly, "Back to your places."

They returned to their desks, quiet and shocked.

"Will you work on your own?" asked the teacher. "I have to leave you for a moment."

Arnold whispered to Piet, "Why did they take them?"

"No idea. Been up to something, no doubt. If you ask me, they've picked just the right ones."

"What do you mean?"

"All boys with rich fathers! All flashy types who think they know it all!"

"Do you know them well?"

"One or two. My father was saying only yesterday that it was time some of them were taught a lesson."

Vague suspicions began to form in Arnold's mind, but he did not dare to voice them. He only asked, "Did your father work late last night?"

"I don't know. Why?"

"Oh, no reason."

Mr. Geurtsen returned. The class was quiet at once. "A German reprisal," he said curtly, "because of General Seyffardt's murder. They've taken twelve boys." He stopped for a moment and then went on quietly, "The head has therefore decided to close the school this afternoon."

No cheering this time, just muffled whispers.

Again Arnold felt the suffocating tension rise in him as he

hurried home at lunchtime. Somehow he felt almost guilty. What could the boys have done? What had Frerk Wiersema on his conscience? What would happen to them now?

At the table he said, "They took twelve boys away from school this morning, in police vans."

Mr. Westervoort did not react.

"Frerk Wiersema was one of them."

"Frerk Wiersema?" asked Rita. "Who's he?"

"He was skating that day—you know. Geurtsen said they did it because of General Seyffardt having been shot. A reprisal. Is that true?"

"This Geurtsen—is he the one who teaches you German now?"

"Yes."

"What gave him that idea?"

"He went to ask. And we've got the afternoon off."

"Off? Why?"

"School's closed because of the twelve boys."

Mr. Westervoort banged down his knife and fork and slammed his fist on the table. "What's this? School closed because a group of agitators from the exploiting classes has been picked up? This is the craziest thing I've heard yet!"

Arnold did not answer. He was always rather scared by his father's angry outbursts.

"What have they done, Dad?" asked Rita.

"Done? Better ask me what they *haven't* done. Look at the kind of houses they live in: They're mansions! Bulging with money. Don't imagine that others profit from their wealth. Plutocrats like that are asking for trouble."

Wondering what plutocrats were, Arnold said cautiously, "Piet Bergman says they're rich men's sons."

"Then this time Piet Bergman is right."

[126]

"How?"

"How? How! Arnold, don't ask stupid questions. Who else do you think the Germans should be after?"

"But Frerk Wiersema?"

"Frerk Wiersema is as bad as the rest of them. Last night I myself—" Mr. Westervoort stopped in mid-sentence.

"What do you mean by 'bad'?"

"That's enough, now!" said Mr. Westervoort curtly. "We'd do better to get on with the meal. I have to be back at the town hall in twenty minutes."

That evening they heard that another prominent Dutch Nazi had been shot.

As the days passed, Mr. Westervoort grew more nervous than ever. Whenever he heard footsteps on the sidewalk outside, he quickly switched off the light and peered out through the blackout paper. If the doorbell rang unexpectedly he could hardly bring himself to move.

"You work much too hard," said Mrs. Westervoort. "You should take a couple of days off."

"I don't work too hard."

"You're getting thinner every day. I've never seen you so nervous."

"Does it surprise you? Two, three distinguished comrades have been murdered in cold blood! What do you expect me to say—that I feel as right as rain?"

"Koos, be sensible this once. That was in The Hague. You should—"

"I suppose you think it couldn't happen here?" He passed his hand wearily over his forehead. "We must protect ourselves. There's only one thing I should do—I should get hold of a gun."

"Koos!"

"Yes, a gun! What would you say if someone came in here

and threatened us or the children and we had no means of defending ourselves?"

Mrs. Westervoort did not answer.

Meanwhile, Arnold noticed that the hostility toward Piet and himself at school had increased. Boys spat on the ground in front of them and stared at them with hate-filled eyes; they received anonymous threats.

A week after the arrest of the twelve boys, he found a grubby note in his coat pocket: "Your father's dirty work will cost him dear. It's too bad that someone who betrays twelve can only be killed once."

That was when Arnold knew for certain what his father had been doing at the town hall.

CHAPTER SIXTEEN 🔖

ARNOLD didn't know what to do. Did whoever had written the note really mean to do something to his father? Should he let him read it? How would his father react if he did? Would he have more boys arrested? He already had such a grudge against the school and the teachers. Besides— was he really responsible for the arrests? The note said so, but there was no proof. They might be making it all up.

Arnold had to make sure.

That evening he said, "I still think it's a pity they took Frerk Wiersema. He's never bothered me."

His father pretended not to hear.

"And they're furious about it at school."

Mr. Westervoort pushed up his glasses. "You're surely not going to stick up for that bunch, are you? Or have you been influenced by the teachers, too? If so, you must leave that school at once."

"That's nonsense, Dad," he said. "I'm sure the boys were arrested for a reason. I just said it's a pity about Frerk Wiersema."

"Stop going on about Frerk Wiersema. He's just as much of a

useless plutocrat as the rest of them. I've told you that before."

"Is that why you put his name down?"

Bull's-eye! Mr. Westervoort leaped out of his chair, gripped Arnold by the sweater and shook him furiously. "How do you know that?" he shouted. "Who told you? Speak up!"

Stunned, Arnold stammered, "That's—that's what I heard. They—"

"I asked who you heard it from!"

"Koos!" said Mrs. Westervoort, unexpectedly sharp. "Will you stop this! And let go of his sweater. He's only got one."

"He's getting into things that are none of his business!" growled Mr. Westervoort. "And I still haven't heard where he got his information."

"School," said Arnold.

"School, school! What kind of answer is that? I want to know who told you!"

Arnold rummaged in his trouser pockets for the note and slammed it down on the table. "There! Read it yourself!"

Mr. Westervoort picked up the piece of paper and read the scrawled sentences. When he raised his head again, there was panic in his eyes.

"How—how did you get this?"

"Found it. In my coat pocket."

"Who put it there?"

"I don't know."

Mr. Westervoort sought the support of the table. "Can you find out?"

"I shouldn't think so."

Mrs. Westervoort asked uneasily, "What does it say?"

"See for yourself." His hands shook as he handed her the paper. She read it, then gazed wide-eyed at her husband. "Horrible! Who could write such a dreadful thing?" She hesitated for a moment, then said, "But, Koos, I had no idea that you—that you had anything to do with this."

Mr. Westervoort dropped into his chair. "Types like that have to be taught a lesson," he said. "Besides, I was told to."

"But was it absolutely necessary to name the Wiersema boy? Surely you knew about—Arnold?"

"Gea, stop this sentimental nonsense about the Wiersema boy! It makes me sick. Orders are orders! If we all did what we wanted we'd get nowhere."

It was nearly half past eight. They heard soft footsteps outside, followed by something that sounded like suppressed laughter.

Mr. Westervoort listened hard. "There you are!" he said. "Lights off!"

Arnold flipped the switch. In the darkness, Mr. Westervoort made his way toward the window. He was on the point of lifting the heavy blackout paper when a loud bang made the windows shake.

Mrs. Westervoort screamed. A cup fell to the floor and shattered.

Mr. Westervoort stepped backward, tripped over a chair and fell against the table.

From outside came the sound of running footsteps and laughter.

Arnold switched on the light.

His father was scrambling to his feet. "Put that light out!" he snapped.

Arnold obeyed, his hands trembling. Mr. Westervoort went back to the window and pulled the paper aside, peering out in the direction of muttering voices. At last he let the paper fall back into place and turned around.

"Cowardly bastards! No sign of them."

"What's all the talking, then?"

"That's the neighbors. They had a shock, too. Though they have been expecting something like this to happen to us! Put the light on again, Arnold."

Mr. Westervoort passed his hand over his forehead, where a wide, bluish-red stripe was beginning to swell up. "They're unlikely to be back tonight," he said.

"What was that bang?"

"Chinese cracker, probably."

Mrs. Westervoort went to the kitchen and came back with a wet cloth, which she handed to her husband.

"Now you see why they have to be picked up," he said.

The next day, Arnold was in the classroom earlier than usual and heard some boys talking as they clattered upstairs. Johan Laning's voice was loud: "A Chinese cracker," he said. "Left over from New Year's Eve. We had such a laugh! They were terrified!" The little group entered the classroom. "He screamed as if he—"

Johan Laning broke off when he saw Arnold. Red-faced, he dropped his bag on the desk and fished inside it for minutes on end.

Arnold gritted his teeth. So it was Johan Laning. He was always a show-off. But he wanted to know who the others were, so he must wait and pretend not to have noticed.

On February 26, Mr. Westervoort received a letter from NSB headquarters in Utrecht. "In answer to your letter," he read, "we wish to inform you that your problems are receiving our fullest attention. No doubt you will realize that the reorganization of the government will take some time. Your patience will be put to the test, but we are confident that you will bear this trial calmly and dutifully.

"We have, above all, no hesitation in expressing our appreciation of the personal efforts you have made in the interests of our movement.

"In comradeship, for Folk and Fatherland, for Mussert, heil Hitler!"

Mr. Westervoort read the letter with a smile.

"That's what I call writing!" he said. "When you read this, at least you know why you have to stand fast." Holding it like a precious jewel, he folded the paper and put it in his desk drawer. "I *will* have patience," he declared. "For years, if necessary!"

At school, Arnold kept his eyes and ears open but he neither heard nor saw anything suspicious. Johan Laning was keeping a low profile.

Arnold still did not dare to speak to Marloes ter Winkel, much as he wanted to, until one afternoon when he had an unexpected chance.

Marloes was at the top of the stairs when someone shoved her. She lost her balance but managed to catch hold of the banisters in time. Her bag slid out of her hands and bounced down the stairs, books and papers flying in all directions.

"Clumsy!" scolded Marloes. "Now look what you've done!"

She came down to gather up her belongings, but Arnold was there before her. He quickly picked them all up and gave them back to her.

She looked at him, amazed. "Thank you," she said.

Arnold flushed but didn't say anything. He gave her a nervous smile and hurried out of the building.

He saw her again that Saturday afternoon, standing behind him in the line at the baker's.

"Hello," he said. Marloes nodded.

Arnold moved out of the line. "You go first," he offered.

"Thank you."

Arnold let her pass. He felt warm inside. She had spoken to him again!

They moved five feet in the next few minutes. Arnold watched her back, but she didn't turn around. He said awkwardly, "Have you, er, have you done your physics yet?"

She shook her head.

"It's not very difficult."

"Oh."

Silence again.

Just before the entrance to the shop he tried once more. "Er, do you have a lot of shopping to do?"

Again a shake of the head.

"What do you think of—" He had been going to ask what she thought of Geurtsen, the new German teacher, but Marloes suddenly caught sight of a friend on the other side of the road.

"Hey, Jannie! Come over here!"

A girl of Arnold's age crossed the road, stood beside Marloes and became engrossed in conversation with her.

"Hey, you, go to the end of the line!" someone called out. "We all have to wait our turn!"

"Oh, don't worry!" Jannie snapped. "I'm not going to buy anything."

She continued her conversation with Marloes, but Arnold could not hear much of it. It was only when Jannie threw him a stealthy glance and then burst out laughing that he felt uncomfortable. He bit his lip. Why did she have to choose this moment to spoil it all!

Jannie stayed with Marloes until she had handed over her coupons and put away her purchases.

Three or four minutes later, Arnold left the shop, too, but Marloes was nowhere to be seen.

He walked home feeling sad. He could have started such a

good conversation—though maybe it was better this way, he thought. He shouldn't push himself forward too much. At least she had not been unfriendly.

Thursday, March 18, 1943

The whole class was working quietly on a Dutch text, the silence broken only by the scratching of pens.

Arnold smoothed his paper and accidentally knocked his pencil box off the desk. As he bent down to retrieve it, he saw a stenciled newspaper next to Marloes's bag. He picked it up, meaning to return it to her, when his eyes fell on the faintly printed title: VRIJ NEDERLAND (Free Netherlands). He hesitated. *Vrij Nederland*—where had he heard that before? Was it one of the illegal newspapers that were distributed secretly? His father had mentioned them once. Then what was Marloes doing with one? It could only have slipped out of her bag.

He glanced swiftly around the class and slipped the stenciled sheets in his bag, between two books.

"What are you doing, Westervoort?"

Arnold sat up quickly. "Nothing, sir. I was just picking up my pencil box."

"That took you rather a long time, Westervoort. You're not cribbing, are you?"

"No, sir."

"I wouldn't dare, sir," came from another corner.

The class snickered.

"Silence!" ordered Mr. Nijenhuis. "Back to work, all of you!"

Arnold went on working but could not put the stenciled sheets out of his mind. Would they really be filled with foul lies, as his father said?

When he got home at lunchtime he went straight to his

room, took out the paper and sat on the edge of his bed to read it.

It was a small, rather crumpled eight-page newspaper. "NE-DERLAND—ORANJE," was the heading, using the name of the Dutch royal house. "February 21, 1943, Volume 3, No. 7." He turned the pages. An appeal from the exiled "lawful" Dutch government, which meant very little to him, just as he could make little sense of an article about doctors, education and universities. Then an appeal against working for the Germans, a warning to keep silent and a poem about eighteen dead. There was also a piece about German atrocities in concentration camps.

He read the whole paper. It included warnings against certain people, some of them NSB members, which it listed by name. He had never heard of them. Did his father know them? And that piece about the concentration camps—torturing and starving people? He could not believe it. Of course, that was why papers like this were banned: all lies.

Should he show it to his father? No, he would ask at once where Arnold had got it from. Should he return it to Marloes? Put it quietly back in her bag?—no one need see.

But the concentration camp article stuck in his mind, and he could not help bringing up the subject.

"Dad, they say there are concentration camps in Germany. Is that true?"

"Who says so?"

"Oh, I don't know—I just heard it. Isn't it true, then?"

"If by concentration camps you mean institutions where criminals and so on are shut up for a while, then it's true. But they're not just in Germany; they're here, too."

"And is it true that they torture people there?"

"Torture? Whatever gave you that idea?"

"I thought they did."

Mr. Westervoort answered calmly, "Then you thought wrong. They don't torture people. They reeducate the prisoners and put them to work. Concentration camps are for degenerates and loafers. Good thing, too: It's a way of separating the scum from healthy, normal people who work with pleasure and a sense of responsibility."

"What about the Jews—are they there, too?"

"The Jews? Of course they are! We should have driven them out of the country much sooner. Wherever they have gone, the Jews have made trouble; they've exploited people and abused their hospitality. The concentration camps at last give them a chance to work for us."

Arnold nodded. So they *were* lies in the paper. How could Marloes read such stuff, and believe it, too? Should he tell her?

He turned it over in his mind. On Sunday afternoon he walked for hours along the river and through the streets, hoping to bump into her.

When he came home at last, he could feel at once that something was wrong.

"Where have you been?" asked Mr. Westervoort.

"Walking. Why?"

"Whose house have you been to?"

"I haven't been to anyone's house," he replied in amazement. "What's the matter?"

"This is the matter!" Mr. Westervoort slapped a crumpled newspaper down on the table.

Arnold recognized it at once; he felt he was sinking into the ground.

"That—that—how—" he stammered.

"How did you get this?" Mr. Westervoort's voice trembled with pent-up anger.

"It—it isn't mine."

"That's not what I asked—I asked how you got it!"

"I found—"

"Found!" Mr. Westervoort laughed derisively. "You find the strangest things! For the last time—where did you get this dirty, disgusting reading matter?"

"I've just told you—I found it."

"You're lying!" Mr. Westervoort broke in. "You didn't find it at all. Someone gave it to you, to poison you and us with lies and false propaganda! Speak up—who was it?"

Arnold's knees knocked. Should he say that the paper came from Marloes ter Winkel's bag? What would happen to her? Would his father—

"Are you going to tell me?" Mr. Westervoort gripped his shoulders. It hurt. "Or must I hit you?"

Arnold swallowed with difficulty. "Johan Laning," he said. "I took it out of Johan Laning's bag. I meant to give it to you, but—I forgot."

Mr. Westervoort let go of his son. "So, Johan Laning. Is he in your class?"

"Yes."

"Why didn't you tell me before? Did you want to protect him, like that Wiersema boy?"

Arnold shook his head.

"You realize, of course, that I cannot let a thing like this pass. Johan Laning hasn't heard the last of this. And you—you won't leave the house all week!" He took the paper and tore it into shreds. Then he opened the stove door and threw it in.

Within seconds, *Vrij Nederland* had gone up in flames.

[138]

CHAPTER SEVENTEEN

A COUPLE of weeks went by. Mr. Westervoort had a new job, reorganizing the rationing office, and came home late every evening, bringing piles of paper to work on at home.

"I never saw such a pigsty," he sighed. "And then there are all those changes. Hardly a day goes by without the rations being changed. And the staff—I've seldom seen such a lazy group! But I'll wake them up! They've got to work, and hard."

"As long as you don't overwork yourself."

"No one's yet been sick through overwork."

Meanwhile, Arnold was daily expecting Johan Laning to be arrested. When nothing happened, he began to wonder if his father had forgotten. It was quite possible, given the pressure of his new job. Should he remind him? Only—you never knew how he would react. It might also remind him that he'd forgotten to keep Arnold home for a week!

It was probably wiser to keep quiet for the time being.

"Arnold, would you go to the post office for me and mail a couple of letters?" asked Mr. Westervoort.

"What about my homework?"

"Surely that homework of yours can wait? Sometimes I get the impression that you have mountains of homework to do whenever you're asked to run an errand."

"I *have*, Dad. We've got an important German test tomorrow."

Mr. Westervoort hesitated. Then he said, "You must still go. I haven't the time. And hurry up, because we'll be eating in half an hour."

"Oh, all right."

Arnold put the letters in his pocket. The post office was about a quarter of an hour away, and the road went past the railroad station. A group of people was moving across the station courtyard: men and women, children and old people, some carrying suitcases, others heavy bags and rolled-up blankets. All of them had a yellow star on their chests. Jews!

They trudged toward a waiting freight train, escorted by a number of helmeted SS soldiers. A small crowd watched the scene, grim and silent.

Arnold was about to walk on when he suddenly spotted Johan Laning among the onlookers. What was he doing here? Standing right in front as usual, that conceited expression on his face. Arnold slackened his pace and finally stopped at a bus shelter. There he watched the group of Jews being led through the gate.

A girl of about six dropped her doll. She bent down to pick it up, but a German boot got there first: The doll flew across the ground. The spectators froze. Except for Johan Laning. He ran forward, grabbed the doll, pushed his way through and gave it back to the child.

For a moment the SS soldiers seemed only amazed at the boy's impudence. Then one of them swung up his gun.

The butt hit Johan Laning in the chest. He staggered backward with a hoarse cry, stumbled over the curb and fell, banging his head against the sidewalk. He lay quite still.

Almost a minute passed before one of the spectators walked to him and bent over him. By then the Germans were busy loading their prisoners. Arnold stayed there until a stretcher was brought out of the station; the men lifted the motionless body and covered it with a gray blanket.

As they carried Johan Laning away, Arnold's glance slid over the train. He caught a glimpse of a satisfied little face in one of the door openings and little hands clutching a doll. Then the wagons were locked.

He walked home in confusion.

"You were quick," said Mr. Westervoort.

"What . . . ?"

"I said, you were quick. You must have run. Had the six o'clock pickup already gone?"

"Pickup? Oh!" Arnold clapped his hand to his mouth.

"What is it? You have mailed the letters, haven't you?"

Arnold stared at his father in total bewilderment. "I forgot."

"You forgot? I send you to the post office to mail a couple of letters—and you forget? Where are your brains?"

"I'll go back again. . . ."

"You certainly will!"

"But the food's on the table," said Mrs. Westervoort.

"No matter! The idiot has to be taught to do as he's told!"

Arnold did not even hear the last bit. He had already left their street and was running in the direction of the post office.

Ten minutes later the letters were in the box.

As he passed the station for the third time on his way home, the freight train was moving off in an easterly direction.

Friday, April 30, 1943

Arnold was the first to hear the noise outside the school. A loud voice reached them, followed by noisy cheering.

Mr. Nijenhuis said, "Stay quietly in your seats. I'll see what's going on."

He might just as well have been talking to the desks, for in a flash all the students were jostling for position at the small windows. The street was full of men and more kept coming.

"They're coming from the factory next door," said someone.

"From there, too!" shouted another, pointing. "Lot's more! All the factories seem to be emptying!"

"Maybe they've got the day off," said Marloes. She was standing next to Arnold, who hardly dared to move.

"The day off?" Hans van Beek jeered. "Don't be so naïve. Workers never have days off. If you ask me, they're on strike. My father said something about it this morning."

"Can't we join them?" someone asked. "After all, we're in a factory, too."

"Look—juniors!" shouted Hans van Beek again. "They're walking with them. I'm going, too!" He ran to the door, but Mr. Nijenhuis was there first.

"You'll do nothing of the sort!"

"Why not? Everyone's down there."

"You don't even know what it's about."

Onno van Dijk suddenly said, "I do, sir. *They* want to make all Dutch soldiers prisoners of war."

Mr. Nijenhuis's mouth tightened. "Exactly! And that is exactly why you are all staying here. It's much too dangerous in the streets. Who knows what might happen!"

"We're going on strike, too," cried Marloes.

"Don't do that," Arnold warned her. "It's much too dangerous. The Germans will be along soon—"

"Don't interfere!" she snapped at him. "You just be a good boy and do as the Germans say."

"That's not what I meant. If they find out that we—"

"Oh, bug off!"

Arnold fell silent, confused. Why was she so angry? Surely he hadn't said anything wrong?

He said to Piet Bergman, "The strike will never work. The Germans won't have it!"

"They'll find that out soon enough."

The class was uncontrollable. To top it all, one of the boys from another class threw open the door and announced, "We're striking, too!"

Mr. Nijenhuis was almost trampled underfoot when he tried to stop them all rushing out.

Only Arnold, Piet and a couple of others were left behind. Mr. Nijenhuis, exhausted, said, "I don't think there will be any more class today. Just go home."

It was late that evening before Mr. Westervoort came home, very upset.

"They had to arrest them!" he said hoarsely. "The agitators!"

"Did they go on strike at the office, too?" asked Mrs. Westervoort.

"At my office? No! They haven't the nerve, though some troublemakers stood at the windows for a good half-hour. It will cost them; I gave their names to the police at once."

Mrs. Westervoort looked at him, shocked. "Koos, now

was that sensible? You know what will happen to them, don't you?"

"Yes, I know! And they've asked for it! You can't let a pack of troublemakers rule the roost!"

"Did you know them all?"

"Unfortunately not, just two of them: Stegeman and Van de Werf. They and their cronies were shouting that anyone who didn't strike was a traitor. Well, they'll find out today or tomorrow what short shrift the real traitors get!"

Arnold said, "We didn't have any lessons today."

"What? Were the teachers on strike, too? Which ones?"

"Not the teachers. Mainly the boys from the eleventh and twelfth grades. They just walked out into the street and then our class followed."

"Did you go, too?"

"Of course not. But there weren't enough left for class, so we were told to go home."

"Who told you that?"

"Nijenhuis."

Mr. Westervoort took a piece of paper, unscrewed his fountain pen and began to write.

"What are you doing, Dad? Nijenhuis had nothing to do with it. He tried to stop them going."

"Tried, yes." Mr. Westervoort laughed. "I know that kind of trying. He didn't lift a finger, you mean."

"Yes, he did, Dad. But he didn't stand a chance."

"Of course he stood a chance! Call that a man to respect? Someone who lets himself be brushed aside by a pack of schoolchildren? More like a weakling, a wet rag!"

"Keep calm, Koos," urged Mrs. Westervoort.

"You and your 'keep calms'—it's high time you stopped that!"

[144]

Mrs. Westervoort stared at her husband for a moment. Then she got up and went into the kitchen.

Arnold had the impression that there were tears in her eyes.

The next morning, on his way to school, he saw placards everywhere. Some people were studying them intently.

Arnold attached himself to a group and read with them.

The decree stated that police and SS units would fire without warning on assemblies of any kind, or gatherings of more than five people in public places. A curfew was imposed from 8:00 P.M. to 6:00 A.M. No alcohol was to be served or drunk on public premises, and its sale and purchase were declared illegal. Employers were forbidden to pay strikers for days or hours missed. Stores that failed to open at the prescribed or customary times would be seized by the SD, the German security police.

Someone looked around. "Gatherings of more than five people," he observed. "Then we're in danger. There are already six of us!"

The man beside him grinned. "They could just shoot you," he said, "then we'll be five again." When he noticed that his remark had not been too well received he slipped away.

That Saturday morning, Arnold arrived at a school that was closed. The other factory buildings in the street were also deserted.

While he was wondering what to do, a German armored car turned into the street and raced past him. The four heavily armed soldiers on top paid no attention to him.

Arnold ran into two of his classmates on his way home.

"School's closed," he said.

"*What* a shame!" said one. The boys sauntered on.

Arnold went home, via the marketplace. Despite the ban,

people were talking in groups. A dozen men came out of a side street, obviously about to cross the square in the direction of the factories, when the armored car suddenly reappeared.

The men reacted quickly. Some ducked down an alleyway, others raced across the square.

A machine gun began to rattle. Bullets smashed into gables and storefronts. Windows shattered. People screamed.

Arnold instinctively dropped to the ground. The armored car swept the marketplace clear and headed toward the industrial area.

Arnold raised his head. The square was empty now, but for one man lying on the other side, his head snapped sideways, his arms unnaturally bent. He was not moving.

Arnold felt cold and clammy. Getting up was an effort, as if he had been lying awkwardly on the ground for hours. He broke into a run.

That same evening more placards appeared. This time the words were different:

DEATH PENALTY
For infringement of the EMERGENCY REGULATIONS,
the following have been condemned to death by summary procedure:
Gerrit Jan STEGEMAN, factory worker
Pieter VAN DE WERF, mechanic
Frederik BROERE, mechanic
for failing to report for work.
THE THREE SENTENCES WILL BE CARRIED OUT BY FIRING SQUAD

May 1, 1943
Supreme SS and Police Chief
in the Netherlands
signed: RAUTER
ss Gruppenführer and
Lt.-Gen. of Police.

[146]

CHAPTER EIGHTEEN ✍

THE strike was broken.

Mr. Westervoort was pleased. Or rather, he should have been. Instead, he was restless and seemed hunted.

"Are you feeling all right, Koos?" asked Mrs. Westervoort.

"What? Yes, I feel fine."

"Is something bothering you?" she persisted. "That threatening letter, maybe?"

"That! That was more than three months ago."

"Is it something to do with the strike, then?"

"The strike's over," he said curtly. "And I don't want to hear another word about it! It's all over and done with!"

This time Mrs. Westervoort refused to be put off. "Do you mean you wouldn't have said anything if you'd known?"

"I don't know what you're talking about."

"Those two men," she said quietly, "Stegeman and Van de Werf."

"Didn't I say I didn't want to hear another word about it? They would have been arrested anyway."

"How do you know?"

"Do you really think the police would have ignored the two biggest agitators in town? Come on now."

"Then you need not have—" Mrs. Westervoort began.

"What is this?" he broke in. "A trial? Do I have to justify my actions to you? Those fellows got what they deserved!"

Mrs. Westervoort stood staring at her husband.

"They knew what to expect!" he continued heatedly. "The fools! And yet they stayed out on strike, went on stirring up trouble! As if dedication and duty meant nothing. And in time of war, too! While millions of Germans are sacrificing themselves in the fight against Bolshevism!"

There was an oppressive silence.

"Is everything different in wartime, then?" she asked. "Is normal justice no longer possible?"

"Normal justice my foot! We are in a state of emergency now. That's clear enough. We will stand for no more nonsense!"

"But what if people think differently?"

"Anyone who thinks differently is wrong and a danger to society. Gea, understand this once and for all: If everyone went his own way, there would be a complete shambles. We must have authority. And leadership. A nation without a leader is a house of cards that collapses in the first puff of wind."

Mr. Westervoort passed his hand wearily over his forehead. "Gea, we've been through this so often—why do you go on doubting?"

"I don't know, Koos. But this war—it's all so terrible, and sometimes I'm so afraid."

Mr. Westervoort drew his wife to him.

"That isn't necessary, Gea. You have to believe in the future, because the future is ours. We will live in a world at peace, in a country without poverty, our Fatherland, where everyone will be happy!"

Arnold listened to his father, but he did not know what to

[148]

think. He said cautiously, "Dad, what if people who think differently are in the majority? I mean, not everyone is a member of the NSB."

"Are you going to start now, too, Arnold? Why do you think all these measures have to be taken, if not for our own good? You surely don't doubt that our Leader wants the best for our people, our Fatherland? And who says that what the majority thinks is right? Yes, maybe the types who still believe in democracy. But you know as well as I do that those days are over."

Arnold was silent. In his mind he could see the motionless figure in the market square. What had he actually done? Been on strike, perhaps, or maybe not even that. Perhaps he just happened to be walking across the square, like Arnold himself. Had he been sacrificed for the common good? And the three men who had been executed by firing squad—had they stood in the way of future happiness? What kind of happiness was it, then? And whose?

"What are you thinking about, Arnold?"

"What, me? Oh, nothing."

Mr. Westervoort said, "Remember one thing, my boy: Only a few people understand what it's really about, and know the ideals we're fighting for."

The state of emergency lasted for two weeks. In that time two more men were sentenced to death and executed. Then the Germans had things under control.

At school, various classes were canceled because a number of teachers had suddenly disappeared.

Arnold did not mind at all. In his free time he wandered through the town, once or twice with Piet Bergman but usually on his own. He was longing to meet Marloes. He might be able to talk to her about his doubts, his uncertainty. He waited for her, tried to approach her.

But Marloes avoided him. If he did bump into her in town, she was either just going into a store or walking with a friend. Talking to her at school was out of the question. Quite apart from Marloes's unresponsive manner, he was afraid that Piet Bergman would notice, and he did not want that.

In the month before the summer vacation, all the classes were held in the mornings only. He would normally have enjoyed the arrangement and the reduction in homework. Instead, he felt depressed and lonely.

"Have you nothing to do?" asked Mrs. Westervoort one afternoon.

"Not really, no."

"Perhaps you could help your father. He's always so busy."

"Help Dad?" The idea didn't appeal to Arnold. He visualized a stuffy office and a clutter of papers. "I'd like to go fishing," he said.

"Then go fishing this afternoon. We'll have another talk about it this evening. It would be good for you to be with other people."

"That sounds like fun," he said, "especially since the others won't have anything to do with me."

"Don't talk like that, Arnold! You must try to make the best of it!"

The next day Arnold went to the distribution office with his father. A policeman was standing at the entrance.

"Why is he there?" asked Arnold.

"For security," explained Mr. Westervoort. "A couple of distribution offices have been robbed recently. Not around here, in Friesland. That so-called resistance mob seems to stop at nothing."

After a week, Arnold had the work so well in hand that he was almost beginning to like it. The staff paid no attention to him, but he was used to that. He filled in lists, noted the number of coupons distributed and helped his father check the reports.

He spent day after day at the rationing office. When his father gave him a ten-guilder note at the end of July and told him he had done well, he took it for granted he would be able to leave school and earn even more money.

Thursday, August 26, 1943

It was nearly four o'clock.

Arnold had been helping to cut out coupons all morning. Now he was busy sorting an order of clogs and shoes for distribution the following morning. One of the girls was helping him. The others were at their desks. His father was in the manager's office.

There was a knock at the door and it opened at once. The policeman on duty was in the doorway.

"Are you the manager's son?" he asked Arnold. His face was tense, his arms held tightly to his sides.

"Yes."

"Will you tell your father someone wants to speak to him?"

Arnold put a pair of shoes back in a box. He looked at the policeman, standing almost at attention. Why didn't he ask his father? And why did he stay outside? It was his job, after all.

"Get a move on, will you?" urged the policeman. "It seems to be urgent."

Arnold nodded and went to his father's office. "Dad, there's someone to speak to you."

Mr. Westervoort looked up. "Who?"

"I don't know." He pointed at the other door. "The policeman's just asked me. It's urgent, he says."

"All right. Let him in."

[151]

Arnold went back. "He can come in," he said.

The policeman stood stiffly aside to let through a man whose face was partially obscured by a mustache and a pair of dark glasses. He was wearing a raincoat and his hands were deep in his pockets.

"Good afternoon, young man. Your father's in his office?"

"Yes, sir—this way."

"Thank you."

Arnold looked at the man's back. How strange his face looked—as if the glasses didn't fit properly. He turned around, but the policeman had gone.

"Did you notice something strange about that man?" Arnold asked the girl, who was still sorting the shoes.

"Who? That man? I didn't really look at him."

Half a minute later, his father opened his office door.

"Arnold, would you come here a moment?" His voice sounded hoarse.

The hand that closed the door behind his son shook.

One second—that was all Arnold needed to see what was going on. The visitor was sitting in one of the chairs against the wall. The barrel of the revolver in his hand pointed straight at his father's chest.

"This is your son, isn't it, Mr. Westervoort?" The man's voice was flat and toneless.

"Yes."

"Then will you get the coupons from the safe?"

"But—" protested Mr. Westervoort, "you can't—I'm—"

"Hurry up!" the man snarled. "We haven't got all afternoon. You understand, of course, that your son stays here as long . . ."

Arnold suddenly felt exhausted. A robbery, he realized. The man was after the coupons. Why hadn't the policeman intervened? Or was the robber not alone? Had they overpowered the

[152]

policeman outside? Were there more of them out in the passage?

He wanted to speak but could only produce a hoarse whisper.

"You've got exactly two minutes," said the man.

Mr. Westervoort went to the cupboard full of box files,
reached behind a ledge and took out a key. He moved to the
door.

"Stop!" The revolver moved to point at Arnold. "I don't need
to tell you what will happen if you warn anyone or set off the
alarm!"

Mr. Westervoort shook his head. He was as white as a sheet.

"And remember—I know how many coupons there are.
Bring them all!"

Arnold watched his father open the door. If only he could do
something, warn somebody! The man was facing him. He
couldn't move his little finger without being seen, but he
couldn't just sit there and do nothing, either.

The blood pounded in his temples. "They'll get you!" he said.

"Keep quiet!" ordered the man.

Arnold was silent. The seconds crept by slowly. Wasn't his father ever coming back? Was there something wrong with the
safe? Had someone noticed something after all?

He heard voices in the outer office, followed by orders from
his father.

The man heard, too. He jumped up and came to stand beside
Arnold.

"Don't move, young man! Don't forget!"

Arnold didn't stir. His throat was constricted with fear.

His father returned with a pile of coupons.

The robber felt under his coat and brought out a folded shopping bag, which he put on the desk. "In there, all of it!"

Mr. Westervoort did as he was told. His movements were
clumsy and agitated.

When the bag was full, the man picked it up, put the hand with the revolver in his pocket and nodded at Arnold. "Come with me!" He turned to Mr. Westervoort. "You will stay in your office and do nothing. Absolutely nothing. Understand?"

Mr. Westervoort was standing beside his desk. He said hoarsely, "You'll be sorry for this!"

His legs stiff, Arnold left the manager's office. The girl was still busy with the shoes and clogs. She gave him and his companion a look of surprise. "Leaving already?"

"Only for a minute," he said. "I'll be back."

The policeman was in the hallway, and Arnold saw at once why he hadn't intervened: He was being held up by a man with a scarf tied over the lower half of his face. The holster on the policeman's belt was empty.

"Stay here and don't try anything until he comes back!" said the man with the glasses.

Then they were outside.

"This way." The two men walked slightly behind him; a hundred yards farther on, they motioned him into an alleyway. They pushed Arnold forward until he faced the wall. "Count to a hundred before you turn around!" one of them snapped.

Arnold heard quiet footsteps receding, then the opening and closing of a door, and silence.

He didn't dare to look around. What if one of them were still behind him? He felt both frightened and foolish. "Count to a hundred . . ."

A couple of minutes passed. He turned around.

The alleyway was deserted.

Arnold started to run.

CHAPTER NINETEEN ✒

THE police started their investigations within half an hour. Houses in the immediate area were searched, streets cordoned off. The house in the alleyway which, according to Arnold, the thieves might have entered was searched, but without result: Only an old woman lived there; she was friendly to the policemen but surprised by their visit.

Mr. Westervoort, meanwhile, stayed in his office to answer the questions of a decidedly cool police detective.

There was no trace of the two men. Mr. Westervoort became more and more agitated as each day went by.

"The police are useless!" he said. "All they can do is ask pointless questions. Sometimes I think they suspect *me* of holding up the office and stealing the coupons!"

"They do have to check everything," soothed Mrs. Westervoort.

"Check everything!" he mocked. "Whenever I come across that detective he smirks as if he's glad the criminals have escaped. They should put the German *Ordnungspolizei* on the job. Or their Secret Service. Then we'd hear a different tune!"

[155]

School started again a week later. Because so many lessons had been missed, no one could be tested, and the whole class was allowed to move on to the next grade, so Arnold felt that nothing had changed.

That morning he sat alone; Piet Bergman was sick. Hans van Beek was there, though, and Johan Laning, who had spent four weeks in the hospital. And Marloes, of course. She had found another place and was now sitting in the next row about four seats away.

She was beautiful, he thought, and quite different from the other girls in the class. But she was also out of his reach. She avoided him, just as everyone else who knew who he was avoided him. If only he could convince her that he would not do anything mean. Would he ever have a chance to tell her that he had found the illegal *Vrij Nederland* in her bag?

Marloes suddenly turned her head and their eyes met. Seconds passed; then she turned away.

Arnold felt the blood throbbing in his head. She had looked at him; it hadn't been just an ordinary look, either. The expression in her eyes had been strange, almost sympathetic, but something else besides—as if she wanted to tell him something but didn't know how to begin.

Could she really want to talk to him?

He brooded all morning. Should he speak to her? He must at least try. Perhaps he could ask her if she wanted to tell him something. If she didn't, he could always say that he certainly had something to tell her. If only he could seize the chance—perhaps at lunchtime. But Marloes left the classroom while he was still packing up his books.

He rushed down the corridor after her, but some of his classmates seemed to have noticed. They deliberately dawdled in front of him, blocking the way.

"I know some good vacation work," Arnold heard one say.

[156]

"At the distribution office. You have to be able to get on with people, though, unexpected visitors, that sort of thing."

Arnold vainly tried to squeeze past.

"It's even more fun if the visitors are carrying toy guns," snickered another. He turned around and pretended to be surprised when he saw Arnold. "Hey, Westervoort, did you want to get past? Are you in a hurry? Calm down. They won't do anything to you here. This isn't the distribution office."

Arnold furiously pushed his way through and ran down the stairs. Guffaws of laughter followed him and a voice called, "You've certainly learned how to run, haven't you?"

He looked to the right and to the left along the street. Marloes was nowhere to be seen.

He missed her again that afternoon. He was at the cigar factory gates on time, but she was already on her bicycle. She rode past him quickly on the rattling contraption with its solid rubber tires. She had not even noticed him.

He watched her cycle in the direction of the market, her bag on the back of the bicycle. So she wasn't going home, he thought. And why was she in such a hurry?

He didn't know, and in any case he couldn't care less. She didn't like him. She had made that clear enough.

He walked home, but after sitting there for half an hour getting bored, he went out again.

"Where are you going?" asked Mrs. Westervoort.

"I don't know yet. Around."

"Will you be home late? We're eating at half-past five."

He didn't answer.

"Shouldn't you be doing your homework?" she called after him.

"No!"

Within a quarter of an hour he was at the edge of town. He

sat down in the grass on the dike and looked out across the river. A gentle breeze ruffled the water. A fisherman in his rowing boat tended to his float. To the right of him was the now deserted landing stage. Behind him on the road a bicycle rattled past.

Arnold looked around. His breath caught in his throat. It was Marloes! She rode leaning forward a little, her bag of books on the small rack.

He got up quickly, intending to call out to her, but caught himself just in time. What if she pretended not to hear or see him? He would look a fool.

Marloes rode on. She took the road that led past the quarry close to the landing stage and then turned right into the woods—the same track that Arnold had shown the Germans nearly eighteen months before, when they had been looking for the British pilot.

He followed her into the woods. The track between the trees hadn't improved since Arnold had last been there. Certainly no one would cycle along it for pleasure. Surface roots alternated with puddles, and Arnold was soon wondering whether Marloes would be able to stay on her bicycle.

He followed the tracks for a while until he saw that he was right: Marloes's bicycle was propped against a tree and she was furiously trying to get the thick tire off the front wheel.

Arnold walked the last twenty-five yards with a thudding heart. She was alone at last, alone.

"Hello," he said quietly.

She reacted as if someone had unexpectedly shouted in her ear.

"Er—can I help you?" he offered.

She stared at him, her eyes wide with fear. Then she stammered, "I—I—er—"

"I've often done it," he said eagerly. He bent over the wheel, grasped the hard rubber and began to press it over the rim.

It was a nuisance to do and his fingers got dirty and sore. He straightened. "It's no good. That piece of wire has to come out first. Perhaps we could go to the farmer at the back of the woods. He'll be sure to have tools."

"No," she replied hastily. "No, that isn't necessary. It really isn't. I'll manage."

"You're not going to cycle like that, are you?"

"Er, no. I'll leave my bicycle here and walk. Thanks." She started to take her bag off the rack.

"Do you have far to go?"

"No, only to a farm a bit farther up."

"Oh. Shall I walk with you? Then I can fix your bicycle when we get there."

"It isn't necessary, Arnold. Really it isn't."

He fell silent for a moment, then said, "Marloes . . ."

Marloes fumbled with the straps tying down her bag.

"Marloes, the thing is, I'd really like to talk to you."

Marloes looked up, helplessly. "Not now, Arnold, I have to—I have to hurry."

"Hurry?"

"Yes, I have to, um, to get milk." Her fingers fiddled nervously with the bag. "My mother said I must be back in half an hour."

"Oh." He watched her furiously trying to unbuckle the strap and free the bag.

"Let me do that," he said.

"No!" There was suddenly fear in her eyes. "I can do it myself!" With a final wrench she got the strap loose. The bag slipped from her hands and fell heavily to the ground. The lock sprang open. A pile of papers slid out onto the grass.

They were colored pieces of paper, divided into small bundles, each with numbers. Above the numbers stood the words: CLOTHING, MEAT, BREAD, GENERAL and RESERVE.

Arnold recognized the papers immediately: Lying in the grass were coupons, hundreds of coupons.

Arnold stared blankly at the scattered papers. "How—how did you get hold of those?" he stammered.

Marloes's face was pale and the fear in her eyes had given way to desperation. She fell on her knees and gathered up the coupons, hastily, as if she could save her dangerous luggage that way.

"Those are the coupons from the distribution office," whispered Arnold.

Still Marloes did not answer. She was stuffing the precious papers savagely into her bag.

"Marloes," he persisted. "How did you get these coupons?"

She tried to close the lock on her bag, but it had broken in the fall. She looked at him, her eyes blazing like those of a cat at bay. "It's none of your business!"

Arnold didn't know what to do. Should he tell his father when he got home? What would happen to Marloes if he did? Would they arrest her? Interrogate her, and then, like those strikers a couple of weeks ago—he pushed the ghastly thought away.

He knew why the resistance had held up the distribution office. Thousands of men who refused to work for the Germans or who had not been made prisoners of war had disappeared without a trace. His father had told him a bit about it. They still had to eat, of course, and to eat you had to have coupons. But if they came to the distribution office for coupons they would be arrested, because their papers were inadequate. What was Marloes's role in this?

He said, "Those coupons are stolen."

Marloes jammed the bag under her arm. "What makes you think that?"

He stared at her. "I was there, last week! Two men with guns held us up. They stole a lot of coupons." He pointed at the bag. "Those."

"How do you know that? Did you make a note of the numbers?"

"Make a note of the numbers? No one has a pile of coupons like that!"

"Well, I do!" came the biting answer.

Arnold shook his head. "Those coupons are new."

"So what?" She turned her back on him and started to walk up the path.

Arnold caught up with her. "You must take them back," he said. "Say you found them somewhere."

No answer.

"You might even get a reward for—"

Her face radiated a hostility that Arnold had never seen before. He felt anger boil up inside him. What was she doing, getting involved with the resistance? Gritting his teeth, he said, "What if the police had caught you?"

"Yes," she said, "or an NSBer."

"Marloes," he whispered, "you . . . you don't mean that."

"Of course I do!" she replied shrilly. "Why did you follow me? Why are you always trailing after me at school? I suppose you thought I hadn't noticed? You've been after me for weeks. I can't lift a finger without your spying on me!"

"Marloes—"

"And you've been waiting for me here, too! Well, you've got me now, so enjoy it!" Her voice caught. "Go and tell your father all about it. Go and betray me: Marloes ter Winkel is a courier. She's taking stolen coupons to the people who have gone underground and who would starve otherwise! Then they can arrest me and you will have got what you want!" She hid her face in her hands and burst into tears. The bag fell to the ground for the second time.

Arnold bit his lip hard. "It's not true, Marloes! Listen a minute!" He took her arm.

"Keep away from me!" she cried. "Go away, please!" She tore herself loose and bent to pick up her bag again.

"Marloes," he said hoarsely. "It's not true! I didn't say anything about that newspaper, *Vrij Nederland,* did I?"

She was bowed over her bag, her shoulders shaking.

"If I'd wanted to, I could have told them then, couldn't I?"

"What?" Her red-rimmed eyes were bewildered.

"Don't you remember? In the spring. I took it. I wanted to give it back, but—" He choked.

She wiped her face on her coat sleeve. "You took . . . a newspaper of mine?"

Arnold nodded.

She looked at him in disbelief. "You found it and didn't tell anyone?"

He shook his head.

She whispered, "Why not?"

"Because you—" He searched for words. "I, er . . . I didn't think it was necessary."

"What did you do with it?"

"Burned it."

Marloes went on fiddling with the lock of her bag, but her hostility had gone. "And all this time I thought I'd lost it." She continued hesitantly, "So—you won't be saying anything about the coupons either?"

Arnold stared at the ground. "Couldn't you take them back? I mean—they are stolen, after all."

"No, I can't."

[162]

"Why not?"

"You know why not. A lot of people depend on those coupons, but they can't get them themselves."

"That's their fault."

"It isn't! It's the Nazis' fault!"

"Those coupons were meant for other people. You can't just take them like that."

He thought about the people who would have to wait at the counter for hours. "Those coupons belong to the distribution office."

"All right!" Marloes flushed deeply. "Would you rather let the underground starve?"

"They don't have to go underground. Lots of people report for work in Germany. Nothing happens to them, does it?"

Marloes gaped at him, her fear gone. "Don't be so stupid! It's crazy to work for—for the Germans!"

"Why?"

"Why—why! Don't you understand anything? You don't do work you don't want to, do you?"

"I do if I have to. Everyone has a duty to—"

"What duty! That means the Nazis have us exactly where they want us. Soon we won't be able to do a thing. Would you like that?"

He spread his hands. "But you can't just do what you like! My father says—"

"*My* father says anyone who works for the Germans is a traitor. And NSBers are—" She stopped, horrified.

Arnold twisted his fingers together. "I know what you were going to say," he said bitterly. "NSBers are the worst traitors of all. Marloes, do you really believe that?"

Marloes dropped her eyes.

"I mean," he went on, "*we* want everyone to be all right, too, everyone to—I don't know how to put it."

She said, "That doesn't mean you have to denounce people."

"I never have!"

"What about Moolenaar, last year?"

"That wasn't my fault. That was Piet Bergman."

"Piet Bergman is your friend."

"I only see him at school."

"Not true. I've seen you in town together, collecting for Winter Relief."

"Only once or twice. But I've never informed on anyone. I have . . ." He wavered. Did he have to say it all? Could he trust her? "I have sometimes told my parents how they're always bullying me."

"Oh."

"Wouldn't you have done that?"

"I don't know."

"I can't do anything about my father's being a member of the NSB, can I?"

Marloes's eyes were suddenly alert. "Don't you agree with your father, then?"

"Er, not always. And my mother . . ." He faltered again. What was it he wanted to tell her? He had so longed to talk to her, alone. And now—it was different from what he had expected. He didn't know where to start. Those rotten coupons!

"Marloes . . ." Arnold swallowed painfully. "I thought—we might be able to talk. I mean, at home, my father's so difficult sometimes. And I can't talk to my sister and anyway she's out a lot. Marloes, was it true what the paper said?"

"I can't remember what it said."

"About concentration camps. Do they torture people there? My father says it's all lies."

"Don't you really know anything about it?"

He shook his head.

"Not about the Vucht and Amersfoort camps—how they kick people to death there?"

"Kick them to death? Who does?"

"The SS!" Marloes answered fiercely. "The biggest filth on two legs!"

Arnold thought about Piet Bergman, who wanted to join the SS in a month or two, when he was sixteen. He asked, "How do you know all this?"

"From my father." She was back on the defensive. "Everyone knows it."

"Is your father in the, er . . . resistance?"

Her eyes were dark with suspicion. "My father works at the post office."

Arnold looked sadly at her. "You don't trust me, do you?"

"I have to go now, Arnold. I mean—" She plucked at her fingers. "You won't tell anyone, will you? Nor about the coupons?"

He shook his head slowly. "Shall I walk a bit with you anyway—wheel your bicycle?"

"No, better not. I'd rather people didn't see—" She broke off again in mid-sentence.

"Us together," he finished for her.

She nodded with downcast eyes and turned away. " 'Bye. See you."

" 'Bye." He waited until her slim figure disappeared among the trees. Then he turned and went back to the main road, his mind buzzing.

CHAPTER TWENTY ◢

A COUPLE of weeks went by. Marloes gave no sign of recognition beyond the occasional fleeting smile, but even that was enough for Arnold. He understood very well that there was little else she could do. It would have been too conspicuous if she had begun talking regularly to him, and her fleeting smiles made him feel he was no longer so isolated.

He would have to be careful from now on, however. What if he made a slip when his father was there . . .

Mr. Westervoort came into the room, smiling. "There's nothing to worry about now," he said. "I've just heard that the SD is on the track of the robbers. That pack of criminals won't be able to profit from our coupons much longer."

The shock sent the blood rushing to Arnold's cheeks. The SD—Marloes! His hands clenched, his eyes flitted from one to the other. He looked dismayed.

"What is it, Arnold? Aren't you pleased?"

"What? No, I mean, er, yes, of course."

"I've talked to the head of the SD," Mr. Westervoort continued. "He said the robbery was very sophisticated and that it took them two weeks before they found anything. They'll arrest the criminals today or tomorrow."

There was a lump in Arnold's throat. He had to warn her. He put his hands in his pockets and went to the door. "I'm just going into town."

"What about the Jeugdstorm meeting?" asked Mr. Westervoort.

"Oh, it's been canceled today."

He was out of the door before they could ask any more questions.

In about ten minutes he reached the street where Marloes lived, a wide avenue with golden-leaved beeches on either side. He found number 58, a small house with a steep gabled roof.

If only there were some way to attract her attention without her parents noticing.

There was no need.

A bus chugged past as Marloes suddenly cycled out of the narrow alleyway beside her house. She swerved onto the pavement and set off down the street without once looking in his direction.

Arnold drew in his breath to call out to her but thought better of it; his voice would be lost under the deafening roar of the bus. He had better wait till she came back.

He waited, and as the minutes passed he kept an eye on the rest of the street.

A few children some way off chalked lines on the pavement and started to play hopscotch. Someone in the garden next to Marloes's house began to rake leaves off the lawn. A child of about four trotted along the sidewalk with a little squeaky cart. From time to time the man in the garden wiped his forehead, looked for a moment in Arnold's direction and went on working.

Arnold felt uneasy. The street was too quiet. He would be conspicuous if he stayed too long.

The toddler pushed his cart toward Arnold and looked innocently at him. "What are you doing?"

There! It had started! He did his best to ignore the child.

"Don't you go to work?" the child persisted. "My dad always works."

"Oh."

"Can't you work?"

"No."

"You won't get any money if you don't work," observed the kid.

Arnold turned his back on him and walked slowly away. The boy trotted after him.

"You don't live here, do you?" he said cheerfully.

"No!"

"I don't know you."

"Get lost!" snapped Arnold.

The small face began to cloud over. Finally the child calmly announced, "You're silly!" He turned his cart and ran back.

Annoyed, Arnold left the street. He turned around once more at the end. No Marloes.

Back at home he closed his bedroom door, took out a piece of paper and began to write.

"Dear Marloes, the police know who—" He stopped in mid-sentence and crumpled the paper into a ball. There was no point, he thought wearily. A letter would probably arrive much too late. Besides, what if someone else got hold of it? They'd

[168]

find out that he was involved. Even if he didn't put his name at the bottom of the letter it could probably be traced.

He was startled when the bell rang. He heard someone open the door, and then the sound of a voice. He knew at once who it was: Piet Bergman! What did he want? He had never come around before.

"Are you up there, Arnold?" his father called. "There's someone to see you."

"Coming!" He threw the ball of paper into the wastepaper basket and ran down the stairs. "Oh, Piet!" He tried to sound enthusiastic. "What, er . . . what have you come for?"

"Oh, nothing really. I just thought I'd stop by. There was nothing else to do, and at the Jeugdstorm—"

"Come on up," Arnold interrupted him loudly.

When they were upstairs, Piet asked, "Why weren't you at the Jeugdstorm?"

"No point."

"You're right," Piet answered. "It was tame again this afternoon." He looked around. "Nice room you've got. It's only a bit smaller than mine. You should come over sometime."

Arnold nodded. He sat on the bed, wondering why Piet had come. He asked, "Have you finished your homework already?"

"That little bit? It'll keep till tomorrow." Piet smiled mysteriously. "Anyway, I think I've done my homework for the last time."

"How come?"

"I'm going to leave school."

Arnold's eyes narrowed. "You want to join the SS, don't you?"

Piet seemed taken aback. "How did you know?"

"You told me."

"I'll be sixteen in six weeks," Piet explained.

"I thought you had to be eighteen."

"They want boys, too. As long as you're over five foot eight. Wouldn't you like to join? We could go together."

"What do your parents feel about it?" asked Arnold, dodging the question.

"Oh, they think it's fine. Have you read today's *Stormmeeuw* yet?"

"No. Why?"

"There's a letter in it from my friend. You know, the one who's been in Russia now for over a year."

"Oh." Arnold's thoughts wandered off to Marloes. If Piet left soon, he could still try to contact her.

"You should read it, man!" Piet went on enthusiastically. "Have you got the *Stormmeeuw* here?"

"What? Yes, I think so." Arnold rummaged through a pile of books and took out the paper. The wrapper had not even been opened.

"Give it to me. I know exactly where it is." Piet unfolded it. "Look, here on page 20."

Arnold began to read.

> Comrades write from the front, trusting in God and the Fatherland.
>
> Far from the Dutch frontier, in the immensity of Russia, Dutchmen stand guard, in harsh cold or intense heat.
>
> Quite simply, they are there to protect us from the desperate peril that stretches its claws across the vast steppes toward Europe.
>
> Many have fallen already in the fight. Their last resting place is a heroes' cemetery on a low hill by the Russian village of Selo Gora.
>
> As the months pass, the number of graves decorated with the Iron Cross for valor, or the Wolf Trap, symbol of Faith, increases.

History is being written here with the heroism for which we have been renowned in our glorious history.

We should never forget these men and the heroes' cemetery where they lie.

SS OBERSTURMMANN BERNARD LOSSER.

Arnold looked up. "Is he your friend, Bernard Losser?"

"Yes. What do you think of it?"

"I don't know."

"But it's marvelous, man! Look, I've brought a poster along, too." Piet produced a piece of paper, unfolded it and held it out at arm's length. "Well? What do you think of it? Quite different from all that schoolboy stuff at the Jeugdstorm, eh? My father says it makes a man of you!"

BOYS OF THE NETHERLANDS!

Join the Waffen SS
against Bolshevism—
for the future of us all!

Our glorious forefathers
will accuse us before God if
our people lag behind *now*. . . .

Report to the
Annex of the Waffen SS
Northwest Department
Stadhouderslaan 132, The Hague.

Arnold looked at the poster. "I'm not too keen on fighting," he said cautiously.

"Come on, man, you're not scared, are you?"

"No, but lots of people get killed."

"Of course they do! But did you know it takes ten Russians to down one Dutchman? When will you be sixteen?"

[171]

"In March."

"Would your parents let you come?"

"I don't know."

"You do want to, don't you?"

"I haven't really thought much about it."

"Don't be so feeble, man!"

Arnold shrugged. "I'll see."

Piet got up. "Well, you should know. In any case I'll be finished with that useless school in a couple of weeks." He added,
"You just be a good boy and get on with your homework. If you
think that will keep the Russians away from you!"

"I only said I didn't know," said Arnold, nettled. "I've still got
plenty of time."

Piet smiled disdainfully. "Fine, then wait and see."

Arnold let him out.

Mr. Westervoort looked out of the sitting room. "Was that
Piet Bergman?"

"Yes."

"What did he want?"

"Oh, nothing. He just dropped by."

"That was kind of him."

"I'm going out for a moment," Arnold said.

"Again?"

"Yes, just to the post office."

He walked to Marloes's house for the second time that afternoon, his mind churning with anxiety. He would not hesitate
this time. He had to warn her—or her parents, if necessary.

He turned into the street where she lived, but found it
blocked off by heavy motorbikes. German police stood with sten
guns at the ready. Arnold saw why at once: A gray police van
stood in front of the Ter Winkels' house. A paralyzing shock
made normal thought almost impossible. Marloes! He screamed
inside. They were going to arrest her!

He made a movement as if to walk on. One of the Germans reacted immediately. "Get back!"

Arnold fell back, but kept his eyes on the house until a small, bowed man walked down the garden path and was pushed into the police van. Arnold waited until the van had driven off and the policemen had started their motorbikes before turning for home.

CHAPTER TWENTY-ONE ✍

MARLOES did not come to school for two weeks. When she finally reappeared one morning she looked tired.

"Ah, Marloes," Mr. Moolenaar greeted her, "it's good to have you back."

She smiled back at him.

Arnold sat up straight and carefully avoided looking at her. He had already heard that Mr. Ter Winkel was in prison. They had found only a few of the stolen coupons in his house, but that had been more than enough to convict him. They probably knew that Marloes had delivered some coupons, too. He had heard something of the sort from his father. They had left her alone, but for how long? And what would happen to her father? He thought that stealing and illegal distribution of coupons carried the death penalty.

If only he had been more decisive two weeks ago! If only he had telephoned instead of hanging around like a scared rabbit. He could have warned them then and saved Marloes this misery.

[174]

Piet Bergman nudged him. "Hey, Arnold," he whispered. "Have you thought about it?"

"What?"

"Come on, you idiot. What we talked about the other day. You know."

"Oh—that." Arnold chewed his nail. "I don't think I'll go."

"Why not?"

"I've told you already—I don't feel like it."

Piet snorted disparagingly. "Ridiculous! So you'd rather sit here than—"

"Arnold, be quiet!" ordered Mr. Moolenaar.

"I wasn't talking, sir."

"You were both talking," the teacher retorted calmly, "and you will both hold your tongues when I am speaking."

Piet hissed through his teeth. "There, that's just what I mean!"

Arnold did his best to keep his mind on the lesson, but it was very difficult. His thoughts kept wandering. If only he could do something, ask his father to try to get Mr. Ter Winkel freed. He shook his head. It was hopeless, impossible. His father would not want to try. All he could do was tell Marloes how awful he thought it was. Not that it would do much good. Still, it might make her trust him a little more.

He succeeded in evading Piet Bergman at lunchtime and went to wait behind the wall of the bicycle shed.

He didn't have long to wait before Marloes walked past, wheeling her bicycle.

Arnold stepped forward. "Marloes!" His voice was rough with tension.

She checked her pace, startled, but when she saw who it was her eyes blazed. "What do you want?"

"Marloes, it's awful about your father. I, I wanted to warn you—"

[175]

"What?" The corners of her mouth quivered. "You wanted to warn us?"

He nodded quickly.

She took a deep breath. "You dirty liar," she hissed. "You traitor! How dare you say that—or maybe you thought we didn't know? Everyone saw you watching with that grinning mug of yours when the Nazis came to take my father away."

Her whole mouth was trembling now. "I don't understand why you took so long about it. Did you want to make sure we weren't on our guard any longer?"

Arnold was dumbfounded. "But—you've got it all wrong," he stammered. "I wanted to warn you. My father—"

He got no further. Marloes suddenly let go of her bicycle and slapped him in the face. "There!" she screamed. "Traitor! Dirty NSBer!"

Arnold staggered back. His cheek burned. His voice sounded high and shrill. "It's not true!"

A couple of boys a little way off saw what was going on and ran up, shouting, "Well done, Marloes! Sock it to the bastard!"

Arnold backed against the wall like a wounded animal. He shook his head desperately. "No, Marloes, it's not true."

Marloes stood facing him a moment longer, shaking with anger. Then her head dropped forward. She turned, picked up her bicycle and walked away, her shoulders bowed.

Arnold stared after her but he could see her only vaguely, as if in a bewildering dream. The shouts of the boys around him seemed to come from far away. She didn't believe him. The thought thudded through his head. She thought he had betrayed her father.

"Come on, let's sock it to the bastard!" yelled someone. "You all saw this scum bothering Marloes!"

Arnold's eyes flitted from one to another. There were at least eight of them. Rage boiled up inside him. "All right!" he yelled. "If that's what you want!"

"What's going on here?" The short, angry man was standing among them before they could get going.

"Mr. Moolenaar—" The boys fell back.

"Well? Is nobody going to answer my question? What is going on?"

"This bastard was annoying Marloes," said one of the boys. "We saw him."

"Marloes?" The teacher's eyes glittered. "Where is she?"

"She's gone."

Mr. Moolenaar turned to Arnold. "What have you to say to this?"

Arnold no longer felt any hurt and he made no attempt to avoid the piercing eyes of the man in front of him. He did not answer.

Mr. Moolenaar took a deep breath. "Right," he said quietly. "You will report to me after this afternoon's class. That will be time enough for the investigation."

Arnold's thoughts flew back to a similar moment. How long ago was it? There had been three boys against him then, and the headmaster had intervened. He would get the blame again, just like the last time. Not openly, of course, because they wouldn't dare.

"Arnold, did you hear me?"

Arnold said stiffly, "Your investigation can go to hell." He turned his back on the teacher and crossed the yard in long strides. No one lifted a finger to stop him.

It took him half an hour to get home from school. As he walked down the narrow alley to the back door, he was hoping to keep himself under control so that his parents would not notice anything, but he could have saved himself the trouble, because there was no one at home.

He stomped up the stairs, fell back on to his bed and stared at the ceiling. He would not go back to school. There was no one now who accepted him, not even Marloes. He had thought—hoped—that at last he had found someone to whom he could tell his private thoughts, and now . . .

He rolled over onto his stomach, laid his head on his arms and began to weep uncontrollably.

It was a quarter past six before Mr. Westervoort came home. There were deep lines around his mouth but his eyes held a strange glow.

He went straight through to the living room without taking off his coat, pulled up a chair and sat at the table. "Come over here for a minute, all of you," he said. "I've got something to show you."

"What, Dad?" Rita leaned over inquisitively.

"You'll see in a moment. Arnold, are you coming?"

Arnold looked at him indifferently. "I'm quite happy here."

Mr. Westervoort frowned briefly but didn't pursue the matter. He felt in the inside pocket of his coat and with some difficulty extracted a bulky package and put it down in front of him.

"Look," he said, "a present from our Leader."

"What?"

"You know it hasn't been easy for us recently," Mr. Westervoort went on earnestly. "So few people are aware of the terrible dangers that threaten our people and Fatherland. And on top of that, there are cowardly swine who think they can break us by assassination."

Arnold put his book on the floor and sat up.

"Do you mean the murders of members of the movement?" asked Rita.

[178]

"That's what I mean, yes," said Mr. Westervoort, "of prominent members of our movement. Our Leader knows this, and he knows that it might affect the heart of our movement—so he has not hesitated to take the necessary measures."

Mrs. Westervoort looked worried. "Koos, do you mean—"

"Quiet, Gea. Let me finish. From now on, countless comrades will no longer fall, defenseless, at the hands of ruthless desperadoes. They will show their teeth, just as our forefathers did in the Thirty Years' War! Thanks to our Leader, they need have no more fear. *We* need have no more fear!"

Trying to control the shaking of his hands, he unwrapped the paper.

Arnold got up, feigning indifference, and looked over his father's shoulder. The next moment his eyes widened.

Out of the parcel came a dark brown leather holster that clicked open with a flick of the finger. A dully gleaming gun slid into Mr. Westervoort's hand as if of its own accord.

"A gun," whispered Rita.

With a satisfied smile, Mr. Westervoort put it on the table.

"My God," Mrs. Westervoort breathed. "Koos, why bring a thing like that into our home? It could cause the most awful accidents!"

"No, my dear," said Mr. Westervoort confidently. "Only the inexperienced have accidents with guns."

"But you—"

He raised his hand. "I know what you're going to say—I'm inexperienced. Yes, but I won't be for long. From tomorrow on we're going to spend one afternoon a week at the shooting range."

Arnold took the gun and weighed it in his hand. The butt felt good and his finger went to the trigger almost by instinct. If he had one like that, he'd—

"Give it back, Arnold. Then we can put it away safely." Mr.

Westervoort put the pistol back in the holster and carefully clicked it shut. When he looked at his wife his face was excited. "Come on, Gea, don't look so sad. What can happen to us now?"

Arnold did not care about anything anymore, not since Marloes had called him a traitor. He tried to forget her, but her presence in class made that impossible, although she passed him in the corridor and in the street as if he did not exist.

Even the teachers hardly bothered with him, except to comment on his bad grades.

He managed to keep his grades quiet for a couple of weeks, until his mother came home looking tense one afternoon in January.

"I've been talking to Mr. Geurtsen," she said.

"Mr. Geurtsen?" he answered, confused. "Oh, from school."

"Yes. He says your work's been getting worse recently."

"Oh."

Her voice sharpened. "You've got a German test tomorrow, haven't you? Go and work now," she said, "and I'll ask Dad to help you tonight."

Mr. Westervoort did not help him because he came home late.

"I have to go straight out again to a meeting," he said hurriedly.

"A meeting? I thought you didn't have to go out tonight."

"You know what our Leader said in his New Year speech."

"What do you mean?"

"You know! About the possibility of invasion."

"Are we going to be invaded, then?"

"No, no. But we must be prepared for anything. You never know what the Americans and the British might think up."

"What do you have to discuss?" she asked.

"I can't tell you yet. I only know we mustn't let ourselves be taken by surprise." He put on his coat. "See you tonight. I'll be late."

"All right Koos," she said flatly. "And—be careful."

The next morning Arnold passed his German test.

It was also the day Piet Bergman stopped coming to school.

CHAPTER TWENTY-TWO ✄

Wednesday, March 22, 1944

ARNOLD, would you go on an errand for me?"
He gestured toward the snow blowing past the window. "In this rotten weather?"

Mrs. Westervoort smiled tiredly. "Because of the weather we don't have any coal."

He turned round in amazement. "You want me to get coal?"

"No, just ask them if they'll deliver."

Five minutes later he was walking through the cold, wet streets.

When he reached the office he noticed a piece of paper in the small window. "Gone out. Back in half an hour."

He walked slowly back and sought shelter from the north wind in the narrow alley between the shed and the office. He leaned against the shed and pressed pebbles into the mud with his shoes. He looked at his watch again. Half-past four. If the man didn't come soon he'd leave. Around the corner, near the entrance to the shed, he heard the sound of footsteps.

As Arnold set off down the alley, the end was blocked: a powerfully built broad-shouldered boy was standing ten feet from him. There was a heavy spanner in his hand, and his pale blue eyes glistened strangely. "We've got you at last, you Nazi swine!"

It was some seconds before Arnold recognized him. Then the ground seemed to be giving way under him. Martin Jonkers! His old classmate, who, with his friend Karel Rot, had locked him up in the houseboat, who had threatened him and had finally set fire to the boat.

Arnold supported himself against the wooden wall of the shed. His hands were clammy and he would have run for it, but his legs refused to obey.

Martin Jonkers moved slowly toward him.

Arnold reeled back toward the alley, fear pounding in his head. Martin Jonkers had an iron spanner. He had to get away.

He turned and fled—or tried to, but Karel Rot blocked his way. A knife glinted in his hand.

Arnold shook his head. "No!" he gasped. "No—you can't—"

Martin and Karel began silently to close in on him.

At once Arnold realized that he could not wait another second. He leaped at Martin and kicked upward. The point of his shoe touched something hard. Martin let out a smothered cry. His arm swung down.

The metal scraped Arnold's elbow. A numbing pain shot down his arm. Whirling, he tried to ward off the next blow. Out of the corner of his eye he saw Karel spring on him like a tiger. The knife flashed.

He grabbed desperately at Martin's clothes, intending to haul him to one side, but his nails rasped on raw wood. A powerful blow from the iron tool caught his shoulder. He fell to his knees, unable to avoid the shoe that kicked out at him.

He fell forward, seized an arm and bit into it.

Something cold raked his back. Arnold screamed.

Then he felt no more pain. He saw his assailants leave, Martin limping as if he had sprained his ankle. He tried to get up, but a strange, sick feeling stopped him. With trembling fingers he touched the moist warmth somewhere on his back. When he held his fingers up to his eyes, he was too tired to be surprised that they were dripping with blood.

There was an excited murmur of voices nearby.

Arnold did not hear them.

So it had been snowing again, he thought. Heavily, too. The whole world was covered with a white carpet and he was lying in the middle of it. Strangely enough, he wasn't cold. He was in fact almost warm, but that would be because of his thick clothes and the bright sunshine.

"My God, at last!"

The voice seemed to come from a long way off, as if someone were calling from behind a hill. He turned his head in the direction of the sound and shut his eyes.

"Arnold, are you awake?"

That voice again, now this side of the hill.

"Arnold, can you hear me? Arnold!"

The voice was growing more urgent. He opened his eyes.

A dark shape moved to and fro, grew clearer and finally took on the features of a face, surrounded by hair.

"Hello, Mom," he whispered.

Mrs. Westervoort began to cry.

Arnold looked at his mother, but he felt no emotion. His eyes wandered away, sliding from the snow-white walls to the gray, half-drawn curtains. A private room, he thought with extraordinary clarity. They have given me a room to myself. Why?

He swallowed with difficulty, to get rid of the sharp, dry feeling in his mouth. A nagging pain rose up somewhere in his chest. He tried in vain to move his arms: They seemed to be weighted with lead.

[184]

"I'm in the hospital, aren't I?"

Mrs. Westervoort nodded.

He looked at a bottle above his head, from which a steady drip ran down a tube. The tube ended with a metal insert in his right arm. He asked, "What time is it?"

She wiped her eyes with a handkerchief. "About one o'clock, I think."

Slowly a thought began to dawn. "Have I been lying here for a whole day?"

She shook her head. "You mustn't talk so much, Arnold. The doctor said you must have a good rest."

The door opened. A nurse came in noiselessly and looked at Arnold in surprise. "Well, sleepyhead, awake at last?"

Arnold looked at the friendly face with its pointed, freckled nose. He attempted a smile. "Is it Thursday now?" he asked.

"All day," she answered briskly. "We've been looking after you for quite a while." She straightened the bedclothes and opened the curtains wider.

"I'm so thirsty," Arnold said, "and I feel sick."

"That's because of the anesthetic," she said. "I'll ask if you can have a drink." She left the room. Mrs. Westervoort took Arnold's hand. "Good-bye, son. I'm going now, but I'll be back soon."

Again Arnold could not keep his eyes open. What was making him so terribly tired? And why could he hardly move?

When he awoke for the second time, he noticed that the curtains were closed. A dim light burned above his head. On the locker beside him was a glass with half an inch of water in it.

He noticed that he could move his right arm more easily now, and he tried to pick up the glass.

The nagging pain in his chest stabbed him suddenly. Gasping, he fell back on the pillows. It took him a little while to recover. Then he lifted the bedclothes and saw for the first time that he was bandaged from the shoulder to the hips and that his left arm was in plaster from wrist to elbow.

As he was trying to grasp what he had seen, the nurse came in again.

He gave her an anxious look. "I'm all bandaged!"

"You had to be," she said. "What you've got on is usually enough for four patients."

"Oh." It was a moment before he dared to ask, "Why?"

She drew up a chair. "I'll tell you," she said kindly. "I'll begin by introducing myself. I'm Nurse Wiersema."

Arnold looked at her, startled. "Nurse Wiersema?"

"Yes. Is that so strange?"

"Er, no, of course not. I thought for a moment that—that I knew you from somewhere."

"You've probably seen me in town sometime."

Arnold forgot his thirst and pain for a moment. Wiersema. Could she be the sister of Frerk Wiersema who had rescued him the year before? Would she know *his* name? Yes, of course she would, and nearly everyone in town knew his father.

"Is something the matter, Arnold? You've gone very pale."

"I, er, I'm thirsty."

She held the glass to his lips. He drank greedily. The contents disappeared in two gulps.

"You can't have any more now," she said. "It's not good for you." She paused, and then continued, "You were brought in yesterday afternoon, around five o'clock, by people from the railroad. We thought then that you—well, that it was very serious. You'd lost a lot of blood." She hesitated again. "Someone cut you with a knife."

Suddenly Arnold remembered exactly what had happened. Martin Jonkers and Karel Rot—they had wanted to kill him.

[186]

"The doctor operated. On one of your kidneys. That's why you mustn't drink much yet."

"Your kidneys are near your back, aren't they?"

"Yes."

"My back doesn't hurt."

"What does hurt?"

"My chest and my arm."

"Badly?"

"Yes. I can't reach out."

She said, "You've got two broken ribs."

"Oh."

"And a broken collarbone."

He went on looking at her.

"And a broken arm."

He whispered, "Is that all?"

"Hey! Isn't that enough?"

Arnold laughed nervously but stopped when his ribs protested violently. "I can't breathe in deeply," he managed to say.

"You'll have to," she said firmly. "Otherwise you'll get pneumonia."

"Has my mother been back?" he asked.

"Yes, but you were asleep. And you must go back to sleep now. It's nearly ten o'clock." She pointed to a bell. "If you need anyone, press this. All right?"

"All right. Nurse—"

"Yes?"

"You do know who I am, don't you?"

"Yes, of course."

"I, er . . . you're the first person who's been friendly to me."

She answered gently: "That's my job, Arnold. Good night."

"Good night, Nurse."

When she had gone, Arnold looked again at the bandages. The pain in his arm grew worse. Tears sparkled in his eyes.

Two weeks later, he was moved from the small room to a ward with eight beds in it. They put him by the door.

"This is Arnold Westervoort," said one of the nurses who wheeled him in. The ward muttered a vague greeting. A man opposite looked sharply at him and then began a lively conversation with his neighbor.

Arnold felt ill at ease. For the first time in two weeks he was aware of a hostile atmosphere. And the pain in his chest had scarcely decreased at all. Yet the doctor said he was getting better and could probably leave in about ten days.

Ten days—they crawled by. He had hardly any contact with the other patients. His parents' and Rita's visits provided the only variety.

"The police are on the track of those cowardly thugs," his father told him one day.

"Oh."

Mr. Westervoort looked surprised, then annoyed.

"Don't you care?"

"Oh, yes. . . ." Arnold had already wondered why he had no feelings of revenge.

"I've given our National Guard instructions to watch out for all suspicious persons."

Arnold said, "If the National Guard are all like the ones I met at the station, you won't get very far."

Mr. Westervoort was shocked. "What have you got against our National Guard?" he demanded loudly.

"Be quiet, Koos!" warned Mrs. Westervoort. "They'll all hear you!"

"Well? What's wrong with that? I want to hear what Arnold has to say."

[188]

"You mustn't excite him."

"Oh? And *he* can say whatever comes into his head? Kick our ideals in the dirt?"

"Koos, please control yourself. We're not at home here."

"That doesn't bother me!" But Mr. Westervoort lowered his voice. "I have the feeling that Arnold is the victim of all sorts of undermining influences. He wouldn't be talking like this otherwise."

"How could he be, here in the hospital?"

"Don't you know that danger lurks at every turn? That it can attack us at any moment?"

"I've noticed," said Arnold.

"I don't mean that—I mean the spiritual danger. What will become of our people if they are waylaid on all sides by forces aimed at the downfall of our Fatherland?"

Here we go again, thought Arnold wearily. It sometimes seemed as if his father could not think of anything else. He said, "Is that the most important thing in the world?"

"What about the rally in Utrecht," his father almost pleaded, "you know, with our Leader—"

"That was almost two years ago."

Mr. Westervoort shook his head in despair. "How can you talk this way, Arnold? What has changed you?"

"We must go, Koos," Mrs. Westervoort said hurriedly. "Arnold's tired, and visiting hours are over." She picked up her purse and kissed Arnold on the forehead. "Good-bye, son. See you tomorrow."

Mr. Westervoort gave him his hand. His thin face was tense. "Arnold, we're still comrades, aren't we?"

Arnold lowered his eyes and nodded briefly.

CHAPTER TWENTY-THREE 🖋

Tuesday, April 18, 1944

IT was nearly half past eleven, but Arnold could not get to sleep. His arm was still hurting a lot and the sore place in his chest was painful. He listened to the hospital noises: soft footsteps in the corridor, a door closing, a repetitive cough from another room.

From outside came the rapidly swelling growl of a car engine. Someone changed gear roughly and stopped the car somewhere nearby. Loud voices sounded and someone in the corridor began to run.

He listened hard for a time, but the sounds began to blur, and he was soon asleep.

Nurse Wiersema told him the news next morning. "You'll have company soon," she said, pointing to the empty bed next to his.

"Who?"

"You'll see."

"What's happened to him?"

"He had an . . . an . . . accident."

"What was all the noise last night?"

"I don't know. I wasn't on duty."

She plumped up his pillows. "You can get up for a little while today."

Arnold felt warm inside. "If I can walk!"

"There's nothing wrong with your legs!" She went away and returned a quarter of an hour later with another nurse, pushing a wheeled stretcher.

Arnold sat up and watched them lifting the man onto the bed but even with their professional care they were unable to prevent him from wincing with pain.

"Careful, ladies! Careful, please—I've only got one!"

Surprised, Arnold looked at the young face.

The man obediently rolled onto his stomach and grimaced with relief. "There, that's better. Do I get something to eat, too?"

"Listen to him!" muttered Nurse Wiersema. "Just arrived and he's already after food. You'll have to wait a bit."

"I'm hungry," he declared.

"I'll bring you a bowl of porridge soon," she promised.

"Don't they have bread here?"

"You can't have solid food. And you know very well why."

His face was amused as he watched the nurses leave the ward, but when he turned on his side he seemed to be in pain once more.

Soon afterward he was looking brightly around the ward. "Hello, everybody!" he said. "I'm Jeroen. I'll soon find out who you all are."

Arnold began to wonder if this was the man they had brought in last night.

"What's your name?" said Jeroen.

Arnold looked into the twinkling eyes. "Arnold."

"Can you play ticktacktoe?"

"Of course." He looked at Jeroen, not understanding.

"Fine. Then we won't get bored. What's wrong with you?"

"I, er, fell down some steps. Broke a couple of ribs, that sort of thing." He asked hesitantly, "Were you brought in last night?"

"Yes, by taxi. All free of charge and under armed escort."

Arnold looked at him incredulously.

"Just like a general," added Jeroen. "My adjutant is at the door."

"What?"

"The bastards!" Jeroen exploded.

"Who?"

"The Nazis, of course. I was having such a good time last night and then they shot me in the bottom."

He said it in a way that made Arnold choke with laughter, but he regretted it at once. He fell back, sweat breaking out on his forehead, while the pain in his chest ebbed away.

"You shouldn't laugh if your ribs are broken," Jeroen commented unnecessarily.

Arnold breathed carefully. Jeroen was in the resistance, he thought. They had caught him last night and brought him to the hospital.

"They took out the bullet last night," Jeroen told him, "and gave it to me as a souvenir."

Would they let a member of the resistance just lie there? Arnold was puzzled. He would be able to get up and walk away as soon as he was better.

Nurse Wiersema came in and put a bowl down on the locker by Jeroen's bed. He cast a suspicious look at the steaming liquid.

[192]

"What's that?"

"Porridge. You wanted to eat, didn't you?"

He stirred the stuff. "Call this porridge? It's what we use at home to put up the wallpaper."

Nurse Wiersema pretended to be huffy. "Now, listen, this isn't a restaurant. If you don't like the food, you can go elsewhere."

Jeroen grinned broadly. "What a kind nurse! Today of all days!"

She sniffed and turned to leave the ward, but almost collided at the doorway with a German soldier, armed with a sten gun.

"Where is the criminal?" he asked in German.

The ward turned quiet.

Nurse Wiersema pointed silently at Jeroen's bed.

"The nursemaid!" said Jeroen brightly. "He promised to look in every hour."

The German walked over to the bed, opened the locker beside it and checked its contents.

"There, that's what I like to see!" Jeroen continued admiringly. "Thoroughness above all! You never know what you might find." He offered his spoon to the soldier. "Like a taste? Porridge of the house."

The man growled something incomprehensible, went over to the window and examined the lock carefully. Then he marched back to the door.

Jeroen raised his hand. "Good-bye!" he said warmly. "Regards to your chief."

He swallowed a couple of spoonfuls of porridge. "Lumpy," he stated.

That afternoon Arnold was allowed to get out of bed for a short time. He didn't like it and was glad to lie down again after ten minutes.

"That's quite an injury you've got there," Jeroen remarked. "How high were those steps?"

Arnold forced a smile. "I landed badly," he said.

What kind of man was Jeroen? Did he suspect what had happened to Arnold, or had he heard something from the nurses?

After the Westervoorts' visit that evening, Jeroen was unusually quiet.

"Are you in pain?" Arnold asked.

Jeroen went on staring at the wall. "No."

Surprised at this unusually curt answer, Arnold said no more.

A few minutes later, Jeroen suddenly asked, "Were they your mother and father?"

Arnold's heart sank. "Why do you ask?"

"I've seen him before, your father. In the distribution office. NSB, eh?"

Arnold bit his lip.

"I'd never have thought you were a member of that club."

"I'm not a member," said Arnold stiffly.

Jeroen seemed not to have heard. "And I don't understand how anyone in his senses could latch on to that mob. You must have sawdust in your brains!"

Arnold said nothing.

"Otherwise you couldn't be such a fool as to run after a puffed-up garden gnome like Mussert!" Jeroen continued. "If your dad comes again, I will say so!"

"You mustn't!" Arnold was horrified.

"Why not? He can't do anything more to me."

"Then I'll be in for it," said Arnold.

"You? Why?"

[194]

"My father's very quick to think I don't care about the movement."

Jeroen pursed his lips. "And is it true?"

Arnold nodded.

"Well, that sounds more reassuring. I must say I'd never have seen you as that kind of bloodsucker."

Their conversation was interrupted by the arrival of another German soldier who had taken over guard duty on the ward. He went straight to Jeroen's bed.

"Are you Reinders?"

"Yes, *Herr Obersturmmannunteroffiziersführer!*" said Jeroen.

The soldier's eyes didn't even flicker.

"Where's your wound?"

Jeroen looked shocked. "None of your business!"

"Pardon?"

Jeroen sighed wearily. "All right, then," he said. "Here." He banged on the bedclothes. "On my bottom."

Arnold gave a muffled snort.

The German raised his eyebrows, shook his head and left the room.

"See that?" observed Jeroen. "No sense of humor—that's how to recognize a Nazi." He looked searchingly at Arnold. "I believe you," he said. "You're not a real NSBer. You haven't got the face for it." He pulled down his pillows. "And now I'm going to have a nap."

Tuesday, May 9, 1944

Arnold had to summon up all his courage to ask her.

"Nurse . . ."

"Yes?"

"Have you got a brother called Frerk?"

Nurse Wiersema looked at him inquiringly. "Why?"

"I know someone called Frerk Wiersema. He saved me from drowning once."

"Frerk saved you from drowning? He never mentioned it."

Arnold chewed a nail. "Do you still see him?"

"Who? Frerk? Every day."

"Oh. Thank goodness."

"The Germans kept him prisoner for six months," she said. "We still don't know why."

Was that true, he wondered. Did they really not know? Didn't she even suspect the role his father had played?

He asked, "Will you give him my regards?"

"Of course. Shall I say anything else?"

"No, just my regards."

"All right." She sat down on the edge of the bed. "Do you know you can go home in a couple of days?"

Arnold nodded. "The doctor told me this morning." Strangely enough, he wasn't pleased. What was there to do at home? Here he had Jeroen. They had talked a lot. He had told him all about Martin Jonkers and Karel Rot. And about Marloes.

What would happen to Jeroen when he was discharged? The Germans would take him away, of course. But would he land in a concentration camp, or would they shoot him, like the other resistance fighters? It seemed unlikely. After all, you wouldn't get someone cured in order to shoot him, would you?

Jeroen did not seem to be at all worried about it. "I wish *I* could go home," he said, "specially for the food. They're very sloppy about it here."

"You'll stay here for the time being," Nurse Wiersema said firmly. "You're nowhere near better."

"That's because of the food," Jeroen persisted.

"Well, yes, I suppose we could give you lamb chops," she teased, "or steak with mushroom sauce."

Jeroen cheered up. "I'd prefer a cream sauce, if you wouldn't mind. And the steak rare."

She moved as if to cuff his ear when the German guard put his head around the door.

"Thanks, Heinrich," Jeroen called out at once. "You've saved my life!"

"What?"

Arnold pressed his hands to his chest to try to suppress his laughter.

"Is there a chair in the corridor?" inquired Jeroen. "Heinrich looks tired."

"Be quiet, will you!" Nurse Wiersema warned him. "You're much too sick to say things like that. Don't you understand?"

Jeroen looked hurt. "I stick up for the underdog and again I'm not right!"

She hissed at him, "I mean it, Jeroen!"

The soldier went away.

Jeroen was silent. For once he looked quite taken aback.

Arnold's parents came to visit him again that evening, looking downcast.

Mr. Westervoort took a newspaper from his pocket. "I've brought *Vova* for you," he said.

Arnold looked quickly around the ward. "Do you have to?" he complained. "I've got enough to read. There's a library here."

"I only want you to read this." He pointed to a black-edged obituary notice on the back page, headed by the NSB mourning symbol. Arnold read it.

Fallen in the fight against Bolshevism
for Führer, People and Fatherland,
our dearly beloved son

Pieter Gerardus Bergman

His courage, gallantry and devotion
to duty were an example to his comrades.

We shall never forget him.

W. Bergman
J. L. Bergman–van Hulst
May 2, 1944

"I hope his blood didn't flow in vain." Mr. Westervoort's voice sounded raw.

Arnold saw Jeroen listening behind his parents' backs. He said loudly, "I can come home in a couple of days."

The rapid change of subject startled them. "What? Oh. That's good, son."

"And they'll take the bandages off in about four weeks."

"Good. Then you'll have the whole vacation in which to recover."

"We sent the Bergman family a condolence card." Mr. Westervoort returned to his subject. "We put your name at the bottom, too."

"Good," said Arnold quickly. "Has there been a new stamp issue this week?" His changes of subject were far from subtle.

When his parents left, Arnold felt completely exhausted.

"Who's dead?" asked Jeroen.

"Dead?" Arnold parried. "How do you know someone's dead?"

"I heard your dad say something about it. Any chance that it was Mussert?"

"No, a boy from my class."

[198]

Jeroen made an apologetic gesture. "I didn't know. I'm sorry."

"He died on the eastern front," Arnold said.

"The eastern front? You mean he was in the SS? Was he fighting the Russians?"

Arnold nodded.

"Oh, well, that's different. You can't give me enough news like that. Was he a friend of yours?"

"He sat next to me at school," Arnold replied stiffly.

"They ought to slaughter that lot," Jeroen continued mercilessly.

Arnold turned his face to the wall without answering.

"It's the same mob that does the killing in the concentration camps. String the bastards up, the bunch of them! And I'd be glad to hang on their legs!"

"That makes you a worse killer than them!" said Arnold angrily.

The silence lasted for minutes. Then Jeroen said, much more quietly than usual, "Yes—you just might be right for once."

The day before Arnold was due to leave the hospital, a doctor came to see Jeroen. "What is this I hear, Mr. Reinders? Still running a temperature?"

Jeroen did his best to suppress a grin. "Oh yes, Doctor. I've got a temperature a broody hen would be jealous of. At least 101."

Arnold listened in surprise.

"As long as your temperature stays up, you'll stay in bed," said the doctor gravely. "How is your wound? May I have a look?"

"Only a look. Mind you don't touch it."

The doctor pulled back the bedclothes, took off the dressing and felt the wound.

"Ouch!" cried Jeroen. "I told you not to touch."

"Just as I thought," muttered the doctor. "Infected. Ugly, too."

Jeroen looked at him uneasily. "How bad is it, Doctor?"

"Bad enough to keep your here for at least another two weeks. Nurse Wiersema will give you an injection in a moment."

"An injection?"

"Yes. Any objection?"

"I'm scared stiff of them."

"All the better," said the doctor mysteriously. He turned to Arnold. "You're going home tomorrow?"

"Yes, Doctor."

The doctor looked hard at him. "You two get on well, don't you?"

"You can say that again!"

"Fine."

When he had left, Jeroen said, "Poor old Heinrich."

"Why?"

"He'll have to stay on guard for another two weeks."

"Have you really got a temperature?" Arnold asked cautiously.

"You heard what the quack said."

They want to keep Jeroen here, he thought. There's nothing the matter with him. When he is better the Germans will come for him, and they want to prevent that. But what would happen when the two weeks were up? Would his friends come and help him?

If only there was something he could do.

He pushed back the bedclothes and went up the corridor to the bathroom. The German guard looked sharply at him but let him pass. At that moment an idea shot into his mind, an idea so staggering that it made his palms sweat. Of course there was something he could do! Not at once. In about ten days, when he had to come back for a checkup or something.

They all knew him. Even the German soldiers. They would never suspect him, but he must be well prepared. Nothing must be allowed to go wrong.

Back in the ward, he took a chair and went to sit close to Jeroen. Nobody took any notice.

"I can help you get away," he whispered.

Jeroen sat up straight. "What? But I don't want to get away. I like it here."

"Sshh! Not so loud. I mean it!"

Jeroen looked skeptical. Then he said, "Are you feeling all right?"

"Just listen for a moment. You can't fool me: You're not sick at all."

Jeroen looked impassively at him.

"And meanwhile you're trying to think up a way to escape."

"You've got too much imagination."

"You can trust me!" Arnold said urgently. "Otherwise I could have told the Germans long ago."

Jeroen slowly shook his head. "This is very silly, Arnold. And very risky. I don't know how you could possibly manage."

"I do," he answered. "But I must wait for the right opportunity."

"What are you going to do?"

"You'll see."

Jeroen laid a hand on Arnold's shoulder. "If you ask me, you've taken leave of your senses."

Nurse Wiersema held the injection syringe up. "I admit it—it's horse medicine," she said, "but you need it, especially this afternoon." Briskly she found a spot on Jeroen's thigh and pushed the needle home.

"Ouch! Can't you be more gentle?"

"That's nothing," she warned him. "You'll be singing a different tune soon."

Nurse Wiersema was right. At first Arnold thought Jeroen was putting it on, but half an hour later he saw that his face was beaded with sweat.

"I've never felt so awful," he managed to say. "Everything's spinning in front of my eyes."

Arnold watched his friend anxiously and was on the point of calling someone when Nurse Wiersema came up the ward. She threw a quick glance at Jeroen and left again immediately.

She was back five minutes later, this time accompanied by the doctor and a man Arnold didn't know.

The man looked around the ward. "Where is he?"

"Here."

Jeroen's breathing was heavy and irregular. His face was dead white and his eyes were closed.

The stranger took his pulse. "How long has he been like this?"

"A few days. It got worse this morning."

"What are you giving him?"

The doctor muttered something incomprehensible.

"Why isn't he on his own? Those were your orders, weren't they?"

"All the private rooms are occupied," Nurse Wiersema said quickly.

"Quite so." He moved to the door. "When he has recovered enough to be moved, let me know immediately. I repeat, immediately!" Without waiting for an answer, he left the ward.

It was nearly evening before Jeroen began to recover. "I don't think I've ever felt so rotten," he said. "Couldn't you have done something else? I thought I was dying! What was in the injection?"

[202]

"Don't talk so loud," Nurse Wiersema cautioned him. "It's known as a cocktail," she whispered.

"A cocktail?"

"Yes—a bit of everything. And the creep who came this afternoon won't be back before next week. He thinks you've got something incurable."

"So did I, this afternoon," grumbled Jeroen. "Please warn me next time you've got something like that in mind, then I can take to my legs in time."

"Ah," she said, "if only you could!"

CHAPTER TWENTY-FOUR ⚑

Saturday, May 13, 1944

"SO long, Jeroen. I'll come back and see you soon."

Jeroen almost crushed Arnold's hand in his grip. "I'll hold you to that," he said. "And see if you can find something nice to bring me."

"I'll do my best." Bag in hand, he walked to the door. "See you. Get better soon, everyone!"

A German soldier was standing in the passage, patient and alert. Arnold walked past him to the little room where Nurse Wiersema was writing at a table. "Good-bye, Nurse," he said.

"Are you off now, Arnold? I bet you're in a hurry. Has anyone come to pick you up?"

"My mother, I think, but I haven't seen her yet."

"Come with me."

They walked downstairs together to the hall, where Mrs. Westervoort was waiting.

Arnold stopped. "Thanks, Nurse, for everything. I'll be back very soon."

"Are you coming back?"

He pointed to his arm in its cast. "The plaster still has to come off."

"Oh, of course." She went with them as far as the hospital steps.

"We shall have to walk," said Mrs. Westervoort. "Can you manage?"

"Of course. It isn't that far."

It was more difficult than he had expected. When they got home a quarter of an hour later he fell exhausted into a chair.

Mrs. Westervoort bustled to and fro. "Would you like a cup of tea? I've made some cookies, too. You must be glad to be home, aren't you?"

He nodded. "Where's Dad?"

"Still working. Those coupons . . ." Mrs. Westervoort sighed. "It's almost impossible."

"And Rita?"

"She just went out to do some shopping."

He looked around the room. Nothing had changed. His father's desk in the corner, Anton Mussert's portrait above it, the table under the fringed lamp.

"I gave your room a good cleaning yesterday," said Mrs. Westervoort. "It was thick with dust."

He smiled at her. She looked as if she had aged a year.

Mr. Westervoort came home at lunchtime, but Arnold got scarcely more than a nod. "Things aren't going well," he said. "When I look at the enemies threatening us on all sides . . . And more and more comrades are deserting us, just now, in the hour of danger."

Here we go again, thought Arnold.

"I've just heard that another five members of our movement have left," continued Mr. Westervoort. "Cowards! Instead of taking up arms and fighting to the last breath, they're getting out!"

"I'm going to my room," Arnold said, "to have a look at my stamps."

"Don't stay up there too long, will you? We'll be eating in a moment."

"All right, Mom."

After a week Arnold started to escape the monotony at home by taking long walks. He wasn't afraid of meeting Martin and Karel. He walked everywhere, until he had thought out his plan to help Jeroen escape down to the last detail. It was so simple, but he mustn't make any mistakes. All he had to do was wait for the right opportunity.

The opportunity came on Wednesday, May 24.

About two o'clock in the afternoon, Mrs. Westervoort announced, "Arnold, I have to go out for a couple of hours. I promised to help someone with her sewing."

"When do you think you'll be back?"

"Around half past four, I should think. Have you got something to do?"

"Plenty."

"Good. See you soon."

Arnold went into action five minutes after his mother had gone. He locked the back door, took a screwdriver from the shed and returned to the living room. He sat at his father's desk and imprinted everything he saw there on his mind: the position of the penholder, the pile of books, the papers.

Then he moved everything from the desktop to the table and took hold of the top right-hand drawer.

Locked.

Arnold had expected that. His father had never yet forgotten to lock the drawer where he kept his gun.

On his knees, he pushed the heavy desk away from the wall

from right and left by turn, until there was a decent gap. Then he wriggled in behind and began to turn the screws holding the desk top on.

In a short time he had all the screws on the back loose: Now he could raise the top a few inches without being afraid of pulling the screws out at the front. He wormed his healthy arm through the opening and groped around in the drawer until he caught hold of the holster. He drew the gun out carefully and laid it on the floor beside him. He put the box of bullets in his pocket.

In a quarter of an hour everything was back in place.

Arnold took the gun to his room and put it in an old cookie box he had been keeping in the cupboard. He covered it with a layer of paper and filled up the box with cookies from the kitchen cupboard.

He left the house with the box under his arm. He knew he hadn't made any mistakes. The only thing his mother might accuse him of was eating too many cookies.

The hospital porter nodded and gestured toward his arm. "Checkup, I suppose?"

"Yes."

"All right."

Here goes, he thought. He walked upstairs. The corridor above was empty. There was only the German guard sitting on his chair outside the ward where Arnold had been. He began to open the door nonchalantly, but the German stopped him.

"Wait!" He looked sharply at Arnold and continued in German, "Ah, you're the boy who used to be here."

"Yes." Arnold's knees were knocking.

"What have you got in there?" He tapped the box.

"Cookies. My mother made them." Arnold felt his throat

contract. He thought about Jeroen—how would he get around this one? "Would you like one?" It was out before he could think better of it.

"Yes, please."

Clumsily, because of the plaster cast, he fiddled with the lid. "Let me help."

"No. It's all right now." The lid sprang open.

The solider selected a cookie with care and ate it with obvious enjoyment. "Perfect," he praised. "Just like home."

Arnold gave him a quick smile, closed the box and walked into the ward.

"Ha! Here's Arnold back again! My, you're brown, man." Jeroen sat straight up in bed.

Arnold put down the box. "How are you?" He couldn't stop his voice trembling.

"Bad," said Jeroen briskly. "They still won't let me go. But what's up with you? You look as if Hitler had bitten your ear off."

"I've brought you something," Arnold whispered.

"So I see. Thanks a lot. At least you know what a hospital-stricken person needs."

Arnold looked cautiously around the ward.

"Under the cookies," he whispered, "but be careful."

Jeroen put the box half under the bedclothes and opened the lid. "Mmm, that looks good!"

"No, no, I don't mean that."

"A piece of paper," announced Jeroen. "Plan of the hospital?"

"Don't act so innocent!"

This time Jeroen took out some cookies and lifted the paper. The next minute he was gaping with astonishment. "The devil, Arnold! How did you get this?"

[208]

"My father."

"Did he say I could borrow it?"

"Don't be so silly."

Jeroen nodded toward the door. "What did Heinrich say?"

"He wanted a cookie."

Jeroen whistled.

"I gave him one." Arnold felt in his pocket and took out the box. "This goes with it. Bullets."

Jeroen stared at him for a while. Finally he said, "I was right. You're quite, quite mad."

Arnold was too tense to laugh. "Will you do something for me?" he said.

"Silly question!"

"I told you about—er, Marloes, didn't I?"

"Yes."

"When you get out of here, will you go to her and tell—" He choked.

Jeroen said seriously, "You want me to tell her what we've been through here together?"

"Yes."

"I promise."

Arnold was suddenly in a hurry. "I'll be off, then."

"But," Jeroen broke in, "if your father finds out—I mean—"

"Then we shall have to see." He got up. "See you, Jeroen."

Jeroen gripped his hand. "See you, Arnold." With a grin, he added in a whisper, "You're the least horrible NSBer I've ever met!"

Forty-eight hours later, Jeroen escaped from the hospital, taking the German guard's gun with him. The guard himself was locked up in a closet in the corridor.

Two days later, Mr. Westervoort said, "My gun's gone!"

"What!" Mrs. Westervoort hurried into the room.

"It was in my desk," he stammered, "and now it's gone, and the bullets too. Only the holster's still here."

"How can it be?"

"How can it be? How can it be? Stolen of course, what else?"

"Wasn't the drawer locked?"

"That drawer was locked tight. I never forget that."

"Are you sure?"

Mr. Westervoort started to swear. "What on earth do you take me for? Think I'm an idiot?"

"Where's the key, then?"

"Here! I always have it on me." He took his wife by the arm. "Listen, could you have forgotten to lock the back door?"

"No, never."

"All that silly business about leaving the key on the ledge—anyone could take it!"

"You've always thought it was all right before! Anyway, you're the only one who has a key to the desk."

"It's not difficult to open. Any thief with a bit of intelligence could do it."

"Then there's no need to blame me."

"I'm not blaming anyone!" Mr. Westervoort snorted. "Rita, Arnold, come here a moment. Has either of you had the key to my desk?"

"Your desk key? What would we want it for?"

"My gun's gone!"

"What?" Arnold hoped no one could see his hands shaking.

"I always thought trouble would come of it," Mrs. Westervoort said. "You must tell the police."

"Tell the police? I wouldn't dream of it! How could I ever face my comrades?" He looked at the empty holster for a moment and then angrily threw it back in the drawer. "Wait till I get hold of the scum who did this!"

In the weeks that followed, Arnold tried to behave as inconspicuously as possible. It was not too difficult, because events in Europe were worrying Mr. Westervoort so much that he seemed to have forgotten his missing gun. And when the Allied troops landed in Normandy he grew more nervous than ever.

Meanwhile, Arnold was wondering if Jeroen had managed to reach Marloes. How could he find out? Would Jeroen manage to send him word?

In the end he could bear it no longer. He *must* know if Marloes had been told.

On a sultry July day he went again to her house. The beech trees in the avenue stood motionless. Above the houses, white-edged thunderclouds were gathering.

He felt ill at ease as he walked into the avenue. They knew him here, he remembered. He must try to look like a casual passerby.

He was barely halfway down the avenue when he saw it. He would have liked to turn back at once, but it was too late. How many eyes were spying on him from behind their windows now?

The Ter Winkels' house was empty. The dark windows yawned. The grass in the front garden was knee-deep.

With a feeling of unreality, Arnold walked on. Marloes was not there. Why had they moved? Had Mr. Ter Winkel been freed? Had Jeroen been able to speak to Marloes? His head was spinning with questions.

It started to thunder in the distance, but Arnold paid no heed. He wandered aimlessly through the town until the stormcloud burst. Soaked through and exhausted, he reached home.

"Couldn't you have taken shelter anywhere, Arnold?"

"Shelter?" he asked. "Why?"

The Allies surged forward. German armies were retreating. The fighting came closer. Mr. Westervoort was restless. He stood at the front door far into the night, listening to the squadrons of huge bombers. "They won't get Germany down," he muttered. "They can't do that! Who would be left to hold back communism?"

Arnold stayed in bed. It all left him cold. Everything left him cold if he could not know where Marloes was: his father's agitation, his mother's growing fear and his sister's indifference.

If only he had something to hold on to! But there was no one he could ask. There was no one he dared to ask.

Tuesday, September 5, 1944

"I don't understand it," said Mr. Westervoort. "Why doesn't the Führer use his secret weapon? Surely Berlin can see that they can't go on like this?"

"Who knows what terrible effects the weapon may have?" said Mrs. Westervoort. "Perhaps they dare not use it."

"Any weapons are preferable to being overrun by Bolshevism." Mr. Westervoort went over to the window. "Did you hear that?"

"What?"

"Shouting in the street."

"I'll go and have a look," Arnold offered. He went outside and made his way to the marketplace. There were people everywhere, talking excitedly and waving their arms.

"They've already crossed the border!" someone shouted.

"How do you know?"

"It was on the radio! They say the first tanks are already in Breda."

He wriggled his way through the excited crowd until he unexpectedly came face to face with a group of his classmates.

"Hey! Here comes the sneak!" they shouted. "We didn't even know you still existed. You'll be in for it now, you creep! A couple more hours and it will be 'Run, rabbit, run.' "

Arnold took to his heels, the howls of his former classmates ringing in his ears. He walked down a couple more streets but it was the same everywhere: happy faces, even the odd red, white and blue flag. When he got home at last the door was open.

"Hurry up, Arnold! We've been waiting for you!"

"Why?"

"We're leaving! We've just heard from headquarters. There's a train waiting!" Mr. Westervoort dragged a heavy case out onto the front steps. "Haven't you heard? The British and Americans are already in Rotterdam!"

Arnold stared at his father, bewildered. "What about my things?"

"Leave them! We can only take what is absolutely necessary."

Arnold ran upstairs, grabbed all his stamp albums and flew down again. "Is there room for these anywhere?"

Mrs. Westervoort was in no condition to answer.

"Where are we going?"

"Don't know." Mr. Westervoort followed him out, holding a sheaf of papers. "There are special trains leaving today. We have to be at the station in half an hour."

"Where's Rita?"

"She's still upstairs. Tell her to hurry!"

Arnold looked at the street. He could see more people gathered on the corner where it joined the main road. Then German soldiers, riding past on dilapidated bicycles and mostly un-armed.

"Arnold, what do you think you're looking at! Get a move on!"

They left, he and his father in front, his mother and Rita following. Doors opened along the street. Abuse was flung after them. Someone began applauding.

Arnold felt as if he was going through hell. And where, for God's sake, were they going?

"To the station," Mr. Westervoort said hoarsely.

"Yes, but then . . .?"

"East. The Germans will look after us."

Arnold pointed to a group of rapidly pedaling soldiers. "Are *they* going to look after us?"

"They're regrouping."

Scores of people were at the railroad station, suitcases beside them, their faces anxious, almost haggard. "What's keeping the train? What if we get shot up on the way . . ."

They put their things down at the end of the platform.

The train came in three quarters of an hour later.

Arnold saw the steam engine come puffing into the station. A wild, irresistible idea caught hold of him. "I must go to the bathroom," he shouted.

"Wait! You can go on the train!"

"I'll be back!" He ran around the station building, climbed over a fence and dived into the bushes at the side of the rails.

It seemed an eternity before he heard the train steaming away.

GLOSSARY ✠

Arbeitseinsatz

Labor service required of Dutch by German forces occupying the Netherlands.

Distribution, or rationing

System by which various goods (food, clothing and fuel in particular) were distributed as fairly as possible among the population. Every family had ration books and coupons, which were regularly distributed by the rationing office. In order to obtain rations—i.e., coupons—for the "underground," the resistance had to rob rationing offices or the print shops where coupons were printed.

Gestapo

Abbreviation of *Geheime Staatspolizei* (Secret State Police).

Landwacht (National Guard)

Semimilitary, semipolice organization set up in 1943. The Landwacht was under the command of NSBer Van Geelkerken and consisted of Dutch volunteers who were taken into the Waffen SS.

The Landwacht were among the most hated Dutchmen of the time because they helped track down members of the resistance and confiscated laboriously obtained supplies.

NJS, or *Jeugdstorm*

The youth organization of the NSB. Its members were known as Stormers, and their journal was the *Stormmeeuw*.

NSB

Dutch National Socialist Movement, set up in 1931 by Anton Mussert, chief engineer of the province of Utrecht.

Among the NSB's various ideals were a passionate desire for a Leader, glorification of the "Germanic race" and the creation of a national awareness. These ideals led both to a fatal anti-Semitism and to ridiculous language and strange ceremonies. NSB members called one another "Comrade." After electoral success in 1935, the popularity of the movement waned rapidly, reaching its low point in the war. This was mainly because of the help the NSB gave to the invading German troops and, later, their cooperation in propaganda, terrorism and treachery.

Mussert was sentenced to death and shot at the end of the war.

Ordnungspolizei

Originally founded for normal police jobs (traffic control, water police, fire patrols, motorcycle patrols). Better known during the occupation as *Grüne Polizei* ("Green Police," from the color of their uniforms). The Ordnungspolizei were notorious for their ruthless behavior during raids.

[216]

Politiestandrecht (state of emergency)

State in which the police could conduct a summary trial and the sentence would be carried out immediately.

SD

Sicherheitsdienst. German security service, which also welcomed Dutch collaborators.

The SD was under the command of the head of the SS, Heinrich Himmler (close colleague of Hitler), and even spied on the Gestapo, the police and all Nazis, from the highest to the lowest.

SS

Schutzstaffel. The SS was originally formed as Hitler's bodyguard. Only men of "pure Aryan blood" were admitted. The SS believed (or were trained to believe) that all enemies of the Nazis must be wiped out, so they carried out mass executions of Jews, Poles, Russians and others. They regarded their work and themselves as perfectly normal, partly because those about them did not condemn their behavior.

Volk en Vaderland

The NSB newspaper, sometimes called *Vova* by NSB members.

Vrijwilligerslegioen (Volunteers' Legion)

Group of Dutchmen who fought with the Germans (against the Russians). The leader of this group, General Seyffardt, was also regarded as a traitor.

WA

The "defense wing" of the NSB. Its members wore black uniforms and often marched through the streets. Their strong-arm gangs intimidated and threatened civilians, especially Jews.

Waffen SS

SS department set up by Heinrich Himmler. The corps carried out both military and police jobs and acquired an atrocious reputation. Dutchmen were allowed to join this organization.

Winterhulp (Winter Relief)

National Socialist charitable organization.